BOXCAR KID

Also by Norma Charles

April Fool Heroes
See You Later Alligator
Dolphin Alert!
Runaway
Sophie Sea to Sea
The Accomplice
Criss Cross, Double Cross
Fuzzy Wuzzy
All the Way to Mexico
Sophie's Friend in Need

BOXCAR KID

a novel

Norma Charles

A Sandcastle Book
A Member of the Dundurn Group
Toronto

Editor: Michael Carroll
Design: Jennifer Scott
Printer: Webcom

Library and Archives Canada Cataloguing in Publication

Charles, Norma M.
Boxcar kid / Norma Charles.

ISBN 978-1-55002-755-6

1. Canadians, French-speaking--British Columbia--History--Juvenile fiction. 2. Lumber trade--British Columbia--History--Juvenile fiction. 3. Frontier and pioneer life--British Columbia--Juvenile fiction. I. Title.

PS8555.H4224B69 2007 jC813'.54 C2007-905457-9

1 2 3 4 5 11 10 09 08 07

Conseil des Arts du Canada
Canada Council for the Arts

ONTARIO ARTS COUNCIL
CONSEIL DES ARTS DE L'ONTARIO

Canada

We acknowledge the support of the **Canada Council for the Arts** and the **Ontario Arts Council** for our publishing program. We also acknowledge the financial support of the **Government of Canada** through the **Book Publishing Industry Development Program** and **The Association for the Export of Canadian Books**, and the **Government of Ontario** through the **Ontario Book Publishers Tax Credit program**, and the **Ontario Media Development Corporation**.

Care has been taken to trace the ownership of copyright material used in this book. The author and the publisher welcome any information enabling them to rectify any references or credits in subsequent editions.

J. Kirk Howard, President

Printed and bound in Canada.
Printed on recycled paper.

www.dundurn.com

Dundurn Press
3 Church Street, Suite 500
Toronto, Ontario, Canada
M5E 1M2

Gazelle Book Services Limited
White Cross Mills
High Town, Lancaster, England
LA1 4XS

Dundurn Press
2250 Military Road
Tonawanda, NY
U.S.A. 14150

To the memory of my mother and father
and growing up in view of Fraser Mills

1

A Wild West Welcome
September 28, 1909

Thirteen-year-old Luc Godin stared out the train window. "Now that's what I call a beautiful sight," he muttered, his heart pounding.

Gleaming black bicycles streamed past them in the rain. Some riders were pedalling hard, racing with their friends. Others were weaving back and forth leisurely on the cinder path that ran along the tracks.

"Wheels!" Rita, Luc's eleven-year-old sister, scoffed, flicking back her long braid. "If you want to get somewhere fast, give me a good horse any day."

"You have to admit those bicycles are truly amazing."

Rita shrugged.

"They call them safety bicycles," he told her. "See how they have two equal-sized wheels and a chain running from the sprocket in the back wheel to the pedals? You press down on the pedals, and that's what makes them go. And, boy, can they travel fast! Faster than a man can run. If only I had one, I'd —"

A high-pitched screech of brakes interrupted him. The train was approaching Fraser Mills station, their final destination.

"Not much of a town," Rita commented when the squealing died down.

The train clattered past a bulky building with FRASER RIVER LUMBER CO. LTD. GENERAL STORE painted in large black letters on its side. Rows of small white houses spread out from the tracks to some big smoky buildings and docks in the misty distance.

"That must be the lumber mill down by the river," Luc said.

"Wonder which one of those houses will be ours," Rita said.

"Any one of them would be fine with me." Luc stretched his cramped arms and legs. "I can't wait to do some exploring. It's the Wild West out there. I could speed away on one of those bicycles. Now that would really be something."

Luc and his family had been on the train for almost a week now. It had taken that long to travel from their old home near Pointe-Gatineau, Quebec, across the country to the lumber mill townsite on the banks of the Fraser River east of New Westminster in British Columbia.

The trip had been especially uncomfortable for Luc because of Louisa and Isabella, the two Leblanc girls. Every time he glanced their way they simpered and batted their big dark eyes, teasing him. He had spent the entire week trying to avoid them, which was impossible in the confined space of the train car.

"Finally, we're here," Maman sighed, tucking her blond hair into a blue felt hat. She patted the baby's woolly hat onto his curls and buttoned up his sweater. Then she pulled a worn shawl over her dress. When she smiled at Luc, he noticed tired lines around her eyes.

"I just can't wait!" Rita said as she wound a long plaid scarf around her neck. "Can't wait to see our new house."

"New house, new house," their five-year-old sister, Clara, echoed. She held her dolly up to the window so it could see the new town, too.

Papa was in the aisle, playing his violin as he often did. His thick black hair bounced as he finished the last bars of a lively tune.

"I like that one," Rita told him. "It's so peppy it makes me feel like dancing."

"My latest composition." Papa grinned, his moustache twitching. "'A Wild West Welcome.'" He polished the shiny brown violin on his sleeve, then wrapped it in its special cloth as lovingly as a baby. "Could you put it in the trunk, Luc? It should be safe there until we get to our new house."

Luc opened their large wooden trunk and placed Papa's violin carefully inside. He slipped in his book, as well. It was the most exciting story he'd ever read. *The Adventures of Tom Sawyer*. He had won it at school last June for coming first in English studies.

Maman tucked an extra blanket around the violin. Then Luc lowered the heavy lid and fastened the leather straps securely.

With more squeals and clanks and hisses, the train finally shuddered to a full stop. The porter pushed the door open. The harsh smell of smoke from the engine wafted into the train car and made Luc's nose sting. He rubbed it on the back of his hand as he scrambled around with his family and the other passengers, hurriedly stuffing belongings into bags and suitcases. Luc's seat was closest to the door, so he should be the first out and first to see their new home.

"I'll ask one of the men to help with the trunk," Papa said, pulling on his fedora.

"I'll help you, Papa. I can lift the trunk. Really I can.

Look." Luc strained under the trunk's weight and managed to lift one side of it an inch or so off the floor. He ducked his head when he saw Louisa Leblanc, the younger of the Leblanc girls, staring at him with a smirk as usual.

"If you're sure you can manage ..." Papa looked at him with raised eyebrows. "Let's go then." He dragged the trunk out the car door, and Luc struggled with his end, suppressing grunts.

"Careful going down these steps now, son. Do you have a good grip? Don't drop it."

"Yes, Papa, I have it." The brass handle cut into Luc's hand, but he didn't even grimace. He tensed his muscles and staggered after his father down to the cinder path beside the tracks. Just because he was small for his age didn't mean he was weak. He was strong. As strong as Leo, his big brother, had been.

He lowered his head against the slanting rain and wind and stepped wide to avoid a puddle. One of his boots had a hole in the sole and already the bottom of his woollen stocking was damp.

"How are you doing?" Papa asked.

"Fine," Luc groaned. "Just fine." He wriggled his toes and shifted the trunk's weight to his other hand.

Maman was right behind Luc, carrying baby Joseph with one arm and a big carpet bag with the other.

The path was crowded with disembarking passengers laden with baggage. They were mostly lively young men from around where Luc and his family had come, from Quebec and eastern Ontario near Ottawa. One hundred and ten people in all. They had been recruited to work at Fraser Mills, one of the largest lumber mills in North America.

Another line of cyclists came weaving between the passengers, back and forth across the path. Young fellows around Luc's age. Their bicycles rocketed by on silk-smooth rubber tires soundlessly. The boys weren't soundless, though. They shouted at one another in loud cheerful English voices. Something about a ball game at the park? Baseball maybe? Luc strained to hear.

A cyclist swerved around them.

"Watch out!" Papa shouted.

Another cyclist cut in beside them, heading for Maman. As Luc lurched between the rider and his mother, the cyclist bashed his elbow and he lost his balance, letting the trunk slip from his grip.

"Oh, no! I dropped it!" He lunged to grab the handle, but the trunk hit the edge of the path and toppled down the bank into a ditch.

Papa's violin! It was in the trunk! What if it got damaged! That violin meant more to Papa than anything.

Luc dived after the trunk.

2

Papa's Violin

"*Sacré Bleu!*" Papa's face was dark with anger. "Those darn newfangled mechanical contraptions! They have no business here." He shook his fist at the cyclists and grabbed the other end of the trunk, dragging it back up to the path.

Maman hurried away toward the station, tut-tutting at Joseph to calm him.

Luc stared after the retreating cyclists, gliding away so effortlessly. Such freedom! How he longed to be off with them!

"So come on now, boy," Papa growled. "Are you going to stand there all day? Or are you giving me a hand here?"

Luc wiggled his fingers in the mud under the edge of the trunk to get a grip. He strained under the weight. The trunk felt even heavier now.

"Ah, Le Gros!" Papa called out to his friend, a burly logger. "Come and give us a hand, will you?"

Le Gros turned back. "*Bien sûr, André,*" the big man grunted, dropping his bag on the ground and his bulky bedroll on top. He lifted the heavy trunk like a basket of feathers and helped Papa carry it the rest of the way to the train station.

Luc followed close behind, lugging Le Gros's enormous carpet bag and bedroll. The bag felt as if it were filled with rocks. He struggled to keep it off the wet ground.

When they got to the station, several people were trying to crowd into the narrow doorway.

"Too many people in there," Papa said. "We'll set the trunk outside here under the overhang for now. *Merci, mon ami.*" He shook Le Gros's hand.

Le Gros shouldered his bag and bedroll. "Eh, *mon vieux*," he said, smoothing his beard as he left. "You must miss that big son of yours. Maybe one day that one will grow big enough to be some help, *n'est-ce pas*?"

Papa frowned, the crease between his dark eyebrows deepening.

Le Gros's comment was like a swift punch to Luc's stomach. It was true he was small for his age compared to Leo, but he wasn't that small.

"Josephine. Over here!" Papa called out as Maman struggled through the crowd. Clara clung to her long skirt, looking bewildered. Her hair had escaped from her hat and was straggling across her round cheeks. Rita was with them, a heavy carpet bag in each hand.

"So windy here," Maman said, ducking under the station's overhang, out of the rain. "I need another blanket for the baby, André. Can you get one from the trunk?"

Papa undid the straps and lifted the lid. He pulled out the baby's blanket and gasped. "My violin!" Lifting the instrument, he unwrapped it. The violin's body was crushed and splintered. He closed his eyes and held it to his chest, sighing heavily.

Luc's heart throbbed. "Oh, Papa. I'm sorry. It must have happened when I dropped the trunk and it rolled down the hill."

"It's not your fault, son." Papa patted his shoulder, his eyes bright. "It's those darn kids on their bicycles. There should be a law against riding those dangerous contraptions around busy train stations. Or anywhere else for that matter. How can anyone expect to ride on two wheels like that?"

He rewrapped the broken instrument carefully and placed it back in the trunk. Then he closed the lid slowly, sadly, as if it were a coffin.

The train whistle shrieked through the damp air.

"You stay here, Josephine. Luc and I will get the rest of our bags."

"Can I come and help, too?" Rita asked.

"Of course, *ma fille*."

Luc and Rita hurried after Papa to the train.

When they returned with the last of their baggage, a stranger was talking to Maman. The man wore a dark coat and held up a black umbrella. He was tall and had a thick blond moustache.

"*Je regrette*," Maman was saying, shaking her head. "*Je ne comprends pas l'anglais*. No understand the English."

"I'm very sorry, madam," the man repeated loudly, "but the house for your family isn't ready yet."

Maman shook her head and shrugged. She still didn't understand.

"He's saying our house isn't finished yet," Luc told her in French.

The man smiled at Luc. "You understand English then?"

"Yes, sir. I studied it at school."

"What is this?" Papa said. "*Notre maison?* Our house? She is not finish?"

"How do you do?" The man held out his hand to Papa. "Welcome to Fraser Mills. I'm Dan Rogers, the manager."

"André Godin from Pointe-Gatineau." Papa tipped his fedora and shook the man's hand.

"Ah, the teamster from Quebec. Excellent. Excellent. I've heard about you. We're looking for good men to work with our horses. But I'm very sorry, sir. Your house isn't ready yet. We were so busy filling orders all summer that we only had time to finish the bunkhouses for the single men. The houses for the families are started, but it may be at least a month before we have time to finish them."

Their house wasn't ready? Not for a month? Luc's heart sank. Where would they live in this cold, wet country?

3

Boxcar Kid

Papa shook his head. He couldn't understand English when the man spoke so quickly.

Luc translated for him. "He said they've been too busy at the mill all summer so our house isn't ready. Won't be for maybe a month."

"But what can we do?" Papa asked the man. "Where we will go?"

The man didn't answer. He was too busy trying to control his umbrella as a gust of wind threatened to blow it away.

Maman shook her head. The baby was crying now and she tried to soothe him. She looked as if she was about to cry, too. Clara hid her face in Maman's shawl.

Rita nudged Luc with her elbow, trying to push farther under the overhang. Wind whipped loose cinders into their eyes, and the rain was pouring so hard that big drops bounced up from the ground. Two other families joined them, the Poiriers and the Boileaux, with their baggage and children.

"*Qu'est-ce qu'il dit?*" Madame Poirier asked, holding on to her hat. "What's the Englishman saying?"

Papa explained. His voice rose to be heard above the racket of the train leaving, whistling, hissing, and shunting.

"Mais, ce n'est pas possible!" Madame Boileau cried, her sharp face angry. "They said our new houses would be all ready for us when we arrived. They promised."

"What about the bachelors, the young men?" Monsieur Boileau asked.

"Their bunkhouses are finished," Papa said.

"Maybe we could stay there, too," Monsieur Poirier said.

"My family stay with that bunch of wild lumberjacks? Never!" Madame Boileau declared, pulling her coat tightly around her narrow shoulders. "It's bad enough that our Remi has to live with those ruffians."

It was getting so crowded under the overhang that Luc had to stand in the pouring rain. He pulled his cap lower over his forehead and flipped up his coat collar, but cold raindrops found the back of his neck, anyway. A wet, swampy smell drifted up from the river. Luc turned away from it.

Across the main tracks on a side track sat a boxcar, its broad sliding door wide open. It looked empty and would be dry inside.

"Papa." Luc tugged his father's sleeve. "Can we wait in that boxcar?"

"Let's do that. We'll move our baggage there until we get this sorted out. At least it will be out of the weather."

Mr. Rogers left to direct the group of single men to the newly built bunkhouses. The lumberjacks followed him with their bags, marching away in single file along a narrow boardwalk over the swampy ground to their new homes.

Luc helped Papa lug their trunk across the main train tracks to the boxcar.

"Are you sure you can manage?" Papa asked him.

"Yes, I have it." This time Luc held on to his side of the trunk with both hands under it. His right hand was bruised where the brass handle had cut into it before, but he didn't flinch. The others picked up as much baggage as they could carry and followed them, lugging it across the tracks.

Madame Boileau crinkled her nose as she peered into the boxcar. "It's so dirty."

"It's out of the wind and rain," Maman said. "A good place to wait until they find accommodation for us."

"Heave-ho!" Papa said as he and Luc swung the trunk up into the boxcar.

Luc scrambled up after it, and Maman handed him his baby brother.

"Maman!" Joseph cried, holding out his arms. "Maman!"

"Oh, *bébé*," Luc said soothingly. "Come with me. I'll show you something very interesting." Luc's little brother was a warm, damp lump in his arms. As he crossed to the other side of the empty boxcar, his footsteps echoed hollowly on the dusty floorboards. "See all the spiderwebs?"

The silvery webs were barely visible in the dim light. Joseph took his finger out of his mouth and pointed at the long-legged spiders scurrying up the boxcar sides. He giggled.

Luc showed his little brother all around the boxcar. It was quite big after the cramped train car and smelled good, like freshly cut wood. The sides and ceiling were wooden planks fitted tightly together, and so was the floor. But it was dusty and littered with dirty wood chips, leaves, branches, and bird droppings.

The other children climbed into the boxcar and

were herded from one side to the other while their mothers got branches from a nearby cedar tree and swept the floor like whirlwinds, unleashing their pent-up housekeeping energies. Once they started they couldn't seem to stop.

After they piled in all the baggage, Papa told Maman, "You wait here. We'll go and sort this out with Mr. Rogers, the manager. Luc, you come, too. We might need you."

Luc put the baby on Rita's lap and headed into the rain after them.

They found Mr. Rogers quickly. The manager was the only one in the crowd with an umbrella. He was talking in his loud English voice to the Leblancs, another family.

Luc ducked behind Papa. He didn't want the Leblanc girls to see him. Especially Louisa. She was the worst.

"We've had our busiest season yet this past summer, with so many orders that we couldn't spare the time to finish your houses," Mr. Rogers was explaining again. "We'll try to get them finished as soon as possible, but we still have a big backlog of orders to fill."

Monsieur Leblanc was a big man, big and broad. Looking mystified, he turned to Papa and said in French, "What's the Englishman saying?"

"They haven't had time to finish our houses yet," Papa told him.

"Ah, there you are," Mr. Rogers said when he saw Papa and Luc. "Could you please explain that the families will have to stay in the bunkhouses with the single men until we get their houses finished?"

Papa looked at Luc. "What does he say now?"

Luc translated for him.

"Ha!" Monsieur Leblanc exclaimed. "It was bad enough travelling all the way from Quebec on the train for a week with those wild lumberjacks, with all their drinking and swearing, card playing, and carrying on. I don't think the ladies would agree with sharing a bunkhouse with them for even one night."

Madame Leblanc pulled her two daughters, Isabella and Louisa, close. The feathers on her broad hat quivered with indignation. "If we're forced to stay in the bunkhouses with those dirty ruffians, we'll simply all go straight back to Quebec. On the next train. So they better find some decent place for us to live — and quick." She poked Luc with her long, pointy fingernail. "And you can tell the fancy Englishman that."

As Luc tried to explain to Mr. Rogers, Madame Leblanc stood with her hands on her hips, her eyes narrowed.

"Oh, ma'am, I hope you won't leave," the manager said to her. "We need good strong and hardy lumbermen at our new mill. And we've heard that you French Canadians are really the best in North America. We'll be paying you more than double what you could earn in Quebec, you know."

Luc nodded. He had heard about the excellent offer that had been made. "Could we stay in that boxcar on the side track? For a few days at least until they find something else for us?"

"*Bonne idée, mon fils,*" Papa said. "Good idea."

The manager's eyebrows shot up. "Well, if you don't mind —"

"Mr. Rogers!" a young man interrupted. "Excuse me, sir. You're needed at the office. There's an emergency."

"Yes, I'm sure we'll get it all sorted out," Mr. Rogers said as he hurried away. "Excuse me for now."

"So what's happening?" Madame Leblanc asked.

"We can stay in that boxcar," Papa said. "It should be just for a few days until they find something else for us."

"What!" Madame Leblanc's double chins shook with fury. "They expect us to stay in that filthy thing!"

"As André says, it's just for a few days, *ma chère*," Monsieur Leblanc coaxed her. "It'll be like camping. A nice little family holiday."

"Some holiday!" Madame Leblanc sniffed, holding her wide hat down as the wind whipped at it. "This is disgraceful! I've never heard of such a thing. How will my poor sweet daughters ever manage? They're very delicate, you know."

"Now, now," Monsieur Leblanc said, trying to soothe her while Luc helped carry their baggage across the tracks to the boxcar.

Madame Leblanc and her prissy daughters followed behind in a sulk, daintily avoiding the puddles with their glossy high-buttoned shoes.

"Ah, Thérèse!" Maman greeted Madame Leblanc and the family as they climbed into the boxcar out of the wind and rain. "I was wondering what had happened to you. There's a corner over there where you can put your things for now."

"This is absolutely disgraceful," Madame Leblanc ranted. "Living in a boxcar! I've never heard of such a thing."

"What did the manager say?" Maman asked.

"It may take a few weeks before our houses are finished," Papa said.

"But what can we do?" Madame Boileau said. "We certainly can't stay with those bachelors in the bunkhouses as the Englishman suggested."

"I don't think there'd be room for us, anyway," Papa said. "Some even have two men to a bed."

"It's really not so bad in the boxcar," Maman said. "We could stay here for a few days at least. It's dry and out of the rain. And we could clean it up some more."

"True," Madame Poirier said. She had rosy cheeks and a strong athletic build and was the youngest of the four mothers. Probably even younger than Maman. "It's not any worse than those filthy cabins we've stayed in at the logging camps. At least this doesn't have a dirt floor. And at this time of the year there are no mosquitoes."

"I can't believe they expect us to stay here." Madame Leblanc's lips curled with disdain. "There aren't even any facilities."

"We could use the outhouses behind the train station," Madame Poirier said. "I took my boys there already, and they aren't too bad."

The Poiriers had three little boys, all under the age of ten. They were round little tough fellows with short bristly hair and stocky legs. Clara, Luc's youngest sister, didn't like them at all. None of them would ever play dollies with her.

Monsieur and Madame Boileau had one son, a big fellow named Remi, and he had gone with the other young men to stay in the bunkhouse. He and Leo Godin had been best buddies. The Boileaus also had twin daughters, Bertha and Martha. They were dark and slim like their mother. At ten they were just a year younger than Rita, but they weren't her friends. Luc noticed that they never talked to her. It was as though they spoke a different, private language.

In no time at all Madame Poirier, Madame Boileau, Maman, and Rita finished sweeping out the whole boxcar. All the debris, wood chips, bird droppings, and even spiderwebs were swept out the sliding doorways, one on each side of the boxcar. Then they draped a few blankets for partitions over ropes tied to the boxcar walls.

Madame Leblanc and her daughters staked out what

they saw as the cleanest corner and sat fuming on their luggage with sour looks on their faces as they patted their noses with perfumed handkerchiefs.

"Save that rope, Rita," Maman said. "We'll use it to hang up another blanket. There. That's it. A corner for each family. We'll take this one."

Papa and Luc placed the trunk and the rest of their baggage in the corner. Monsieur and Madame Poirier and their gang of three little boys packed their belongings into the corner beside them. The Boileaus shared the opposite end with the Leblancs.

Maman gave Rita and Luc each a pail. "See if you can find some fresh water for drinking. And mind that it's clean."

Louisa Leblanc peeked over her blanket partition. She wiggled her eyebrows and smirked at Luc.

He turned away quickly and shuddered at the thought of having to spend even one night in the confined space of the boxcar with her and her teasing sister.

4

Lum King

The rain had let up, but the evening was getting dark as the sun set behind a thick bank of clouds. As Luc and Rita walked along the tracks past the train station, four boys whizzed by on shiny black bicycles again, laughing and shouting, their damp hair plastered back and their cheeks red.

"Don't you just wish you had one of those?" Luc asked Rita.

"Papa says bicycles are dangerous contraptions."

"But look at how speedy they are. It must feel as if you're flying when you're riding along. What I'd give to ride one of those!"

"I told you before," Rita said. "If it's speed you want, give me a good horse any day."

"You don't have to feed a bicycle. It won't buck you off, either. And you don't even have to clean up after it."

"Well, a horse wouldn't cause you to drop the trunk so it would topple down the hill."

"Guess you're right. Papa sure was mad. And he hardly ever gets mad."

"The worst part is that his violin got smashed."

"Yes." Luc swallowed hard. He couldn't imagine life without Papa's violin music to drive away the gloom. "Any ideas where we can get water?"

"The laundry maybe?"

"Which laundry?"

"The one behind the train station down along that boardwalk." Rita's sharp eyes saw everything.

The laundry was in a low wooden building. Luc knocked on the door. It was painted black and had a small window that was so steamed up they couldn't see inside.

No one answered, so Luc knocked harder.

"We should just go right in," Rita said. "They probably can't hear us."

Luc pushed the door open, and they found themselves in a small room lined with baskets of clothes. The air was warm and steamy and the windows were misted. Sounds of swishing water and voices came from another room.

"Hello?" Luc called. "Anyone here?"

A young Chinese man wearing a white shirt and pants and a small white hat came in from the other side of the room. He bowed to them, his hands together.

Luc bowed back. This was the first Chinese person he'd ever met. The young man was almost as short as Luc.

"You have laundry?" the young man asked, smiling.

"No. We need water." Luc lifted the buckets to show him. "Clean water."

"Ah, watah. Yes, watah. One minute." The young man took the buckets and disappeared.

"Does he want us to follow him?" Rita wondered.

"I think we should wait here."

Soon the man was back with both buckets filled to the brim.

"Thank you," Luc said, bowing his head again. The man bowed back. Luc couldn't think of anything else to say. He wished he had some money or something to give in return, but the man didn't seem to expect it.

"New family?" the man asked.

"Yes. We just got here from Quebec. On the train."

"Where your house?"

"We don't have a house yet. We're staying in a boxcar for now."

"No house?" The man shook his head. "Stay in boxcar? Not so good."

"It's just for a few days until our house is ready."

"Ah." The man nodded. "Name?"

"I'm Luc Godin, and this is my sister, Rita."

"My name Lum King." The man pointed to his chest. "And I learn the English."

"Good English," Luc said.

The man smiled, crinkling his cheeks.

"Well, we better go now. Thank you, Lum King." Luc bowed again. He gave one pail to Rita, and they lugged them back across the tracks to the boxcar.

When it stopped raining, Papa and the other men made a campfire pit. They surrounded it with rocks on the other side of the boxcar under some overhanging alder and maple trees whose yellow and red leaves fluttered in the wind. The men and children gathered firewood from beside the tracks and nearby bushes. It was hard to find dry bits, but Luc spotted a good armload under a thick bush. He dropped it onto the pile beside the firepit and reached for Papa's axe, which was leaning against a large rock.

"Luc," Papa said sharply, "that axe isn't yours. You must never touch an axe that belongs to a woodsman. To a woodsman, his axe is his most important tool. And I keep that one so sharp that it could slice off your finger without you even knowing it."

"Yes, Papa." Luc had forgotten for a moment how stern Papa was about his axe.

Soon they managed to get a good blaze going under a big kettle of water. Luc and Rita found some stumps for seats, which they rolled close to the fire. The families gathered around and the mothers handed out the bits of food they had left from the train — bread, cheese, and apples. They sipped tea they had made in the big kettle. Even Madame Leblanc and her daughters joined them.

"We may as well be brave and make the best of it," Madame Leblanc said, sighing. She patted her nose with a lace handkerchief and sipped her tea.

Luc got up to get another cup of tea, and when he returned to his seat on the stump, Louisa Leblanc was sitting on it. She fluttered her eyelashes at him over her teacup. Luc felt like pushing her off his seat, but instead he went over and stood with the men.

"How about a good song to warm us up, André?" Monsieur Boileau asked Papa.

"No violin, but we can still sing." In his loud, deep voice, Papa sang out, "*Au fond de ma blonde ...*" The others joined in, and soon they were all singing the lively old folk songs and clapping their hands in time. It was cheerful, but not the same without Papa's violin. And not the same without Leo's loud jovial voice. Thinking about Leo made the song catch in Luc's throat. He took a deep gulp of his tea.

As darkness gathered, the wind picked up and the rain returned.

"Time for bed." Maman led the way back into the boxcar, carrying Joseph, who had fallen asleep in her arms. She made a little nest of blankets for him on the floor beside the trunk while everyone followed her inside.

Luc shook out his own bedroll on the floor beside his little brother. The rain was drumming on the boxcar roof and everything was damp.

After everyone found places to sleep, Papa pulled the sliding door closed. "*Bonsoir*," he said.

"*Bonsoir*," Luc mumbled back. In the dark he took off his coat and cap and boots and made them into a lumpy pillow. Leaving on his shirt and sweater, and even his breeches for warmth, he crawled inside the bedroll and stretched right out for the first time since they had left their home in Quebec a week ago.

What luxury to sleep lying down in silence without the regular clacking of the train tracks! He lifted his arms, lay back, and took a good, deep breath. The air was cold but smelled fresh and clean with the scent of the nearby woods as the wind blew up from the river. He shut his eyes and fell asleep.

5

Luc's Horse Fiasco

The next morning everyone woke at once and the boxcar was filled with the bustle of getting ready for the day. Luc heard some rustling and the squeaky giggles of the Leblanc girls dressing behind their blanket screen. The screen was too close to his bed. Louisa peeked out and her sister yanked her back behind the screen, but not before Luc saw that Louisa was in her scanty underwear!

The back of his neck burned with embarrassment. Keeping his eyes lowered, he stamped on his boots and grabbed his coat and cap. He slid the door open a crack and squeezed out as fast as he could.

Luc took a deep breath of the cold air gusting up from the river. The night rain had stopped, but a thick mist still hung in the air. The oldest Poirier boy, Raymond, followed Luc outside.

"We'll need more firewood for the campfire," Luc told him, poking at the grey embers.

There was plenty of wood along the tracks and in the bush, so they returned soon with their arms full. Although the wood was damp, it would burn once the fire got hot.

"Think this is enough now?" Luc asked Papa, dropping his load on the pile beside the firepit.

"Should be plenty to cook a pot of porridge." Papa blew on the tinder to get the fire started.

Over a breakfast of porridge and tea, Monsieur Boileau asked Papa, "So, *mon vieux*, what are you doing today? What are your plans?"

"I'll go and check the horses at the stables. The manager said they're looking for teamsters to care for them. And you?"

"Me and my son, Remi, and the other men, we'll go down to the mill and sign up. They said we could start work today, so I suppose that's where we should go. What about your Luc?"

"Luc? He'll start with the horses this morning with me. Right, son?"

Luc nodded, but his heart lurched and started to pound. Ever since that terrible day last spring when he was on a cart with his older brother, Leo, and ... No, he wouldn't allow himself to think about that now. Even the mention of horses set his heart pounding like a big alarm clock, making him breathless and churning his stomach. He couldn't finish his porridge, so he scraped it into the fire and put the bowl into the dishpan. Then he concentrated on retying his boots good and tight.

Luc had inherited his mother's slim build, unlike his older brother, Leo, who had been stocky and broad-shouldered like their father. Leo had been Papa's true son, really — not only in looks and lively temperament but in his passion for horses, as well. Luc had never been comfortable around horses. Even before the terrible accident, he hadn't liked them. He'd always felt threatened by their huge presence, their smell, their dangerous heat, their unpredictability. You just couldn't trust them.

"Can I go to the stables and see the horses, too?" Rita begged. She had always shared Papa and Leo's passion for horses, even when she was Clara's age. Rita had the same natural affinity for them that Luc could never understand.

"It's man's work down there," Papa said. "You better stay here and help Maman with the babies."

Rita made a face. She was disappointed, but she didn't say anything.

She sure was lucky, Luc thought as he followed Papa along the tracks, then south across the swamp to the edge of the settlement where a large wooden stable stood. The closer they got to the stable, the more Luc could smell it, and the harder his heart beat until it was thumping in his ears.

At the big swinging stable door they were welcomed by an old man, wizened and grumpy-looking. The odour of horse manure was really strong here, and Luc's heart hammered harder in his chest.

"André Godin?" The old man clasped Papa's hand. "Walter Toban here. In charge of all these hay burners. So you're the horse expert from Quebec. I've been hearing about you. We need a good horse man here, as well as a few more good stableboys."

"This is my son, Luc. He will be my assistant."

The old man surveyed Luc up and down with rheumy eyes. "Bit on the small side."

Papa shrugged. "But he is very good worker. He learn very quick."

"You can come and meet some of your charges right now." The old man led them into the stable. "We have twenty-nine teams of two each and a few singles, mostly Clydesdales. Really the best breed for the heavy work of hauling logs. They're all good horses. Good and big. And much stronger and smarter than those bulls we had in the woods around here a few years ago. Some of the horse teams are up in the woods working now, but you can see the rest."

Luc swallowed hard, pulled his coat tight, and forced himself to follow Papa through the doorway and into the stable. Breathing shallowly now, he stared straight ahead, his hands deep in his pockets, his shoulders rigid. He couldn't let the old man or Papa see how scared he was.

They stopped in front of a stall. "Here's one of our granddaddies," Mr. Toban said. "Name's Thunder."

Inside the stall stood an enormous dark brown horse with a white face. A long mane covered its eyes, and the muscles in its huge body knotted and bulged. The bottom part of its sturdy legs was fringed with long white hairs like little skirts. It stamped its huge front hooves, and the little skirts swayed. Luc grimaced.

"Now this is one good strong horse," Papa said, patting the horse's thick flank and moving his hand along the animal's side. "Eighteen, maybe nineteen hand tall at least."

The horse's bunched muscles quivered. It nodded its huge head, snickering loudly and flicking its tail back and forth. When it turned, it stared directly at Luc with dark brown eyes.

Luc stepped back, cringing inside.

"They all have to be fed their morning oats," Mr. Toban said. "I like to hand-feed them that as often as I can. It's a good way for them to get to know you. Know your smell, your actions. Learn to trust you. As you know, horses always work better when they trust you. Their stalls need to be mucked out every day, of course, and fresh straw spread around."

There was one huge horse per stall, and a row of stalls on both sides of the board walkway stretched away into the murky dimness of the stable.

"More than fifty fine horses here. Excellent." Papa rubbed his hands together. "Here, Luc, you feed this one. And I will get to know these others."

"I'll show you where to get the oats," Mr. Toban told Luc.

Luc nodded and swallowed hard. He followed the wizened man down the corridor between the rows of stalls and concentrated on keeping his eyes straight ahead. But as he passed the stalls he was aware of huge animals snickering and gawking at him. They knew exactly how frightened he was.

"We give each horse one pail of oats in the morning, and they eat plenty of hay, of course," Mr. Toban said. "That's why we call them hay burners."

Luc filled the metal bucket from a gunny sack and carried it to the nearest horse. It was also a colossal creature, brown with a splash of white between its dark eyes and down its long nose. When Luc approached, it snorted and its huge nostrils flared.

Luc crept cautiously into the horse's stall, holding up the bucket. The horse's bulky heat and the stench of manure enveloped him. When the animal's nose dived into the bucket, the sudden movement startled Luc. He dropped the bucket, which clattered to the ground, spilling the oats.

Luc glanced up. Both Papa and Mr. Toban were at the edge of the stall, staring at him.

What had he done! Now he would never get the job. He had disappointed his father again. The smashed violin, and now this.

6

Luc's New Job

"Sorry," Luc muttered. He knelt, avoiding the dangerous hooves, and tried to sweep the oats back into the bucket with his hand.

"You give the horses water instead," Mr. Toban said. "At least if that spills it won't cost me so much."

When Luc held a big wooden bucket of water under the horse's nose, he tried to keep it steady, but his arm trembled under the weight. "Come on," he mumbled to himself through stiff lips. "You can do it. You *have* to do it."

The horse raised its head and snorted at him again, spraying his face with fine droplets. It stamped its huge hooves, big and round as dinner plates. Luc jumped out of the way. Just one of those hooves could mash him to a pulp. Cold water from the bucket trickled down his sleeve. He dropped the bucket onto the ground and hurried out of the stall. That horse could get its own drink.

He tried raking out soiled straw from the stalls, but he was so rigid and stiff with fear that the horses seemed to sense his discomfort. They were restless when he came near, neighing, snorting, and stamping, then flicking their long tails at him.

Finally, at the end of the morning, Mr. Toban said, "André, I can see you have a winning way with the horses and a lot of experience."

Papa nodded. "Grew up on farm. Many horse there."

"Is that so?" Mr. Toban said. "It certainly shows. But that boy of yours … I'm afraid I won't be able to use him. He doesn't have your touch. I've never seen my horses so restless."

Luc was crushed. But he was somewhat relieved, too. He wouldn't have to work with those dangerous animals, after all. On their way back to the boxcar, he tried to stop his face from smiling. "Sorry, Papa."

His father frowned, knotting his bushy eyebrows. "That was a bad accident last spring. You still have scars from it inside. Besides, we're not all born with the same gifts." He squeezed Luc's shoulder. "You'll find something that will suit you better, I'm sure."

Luc knew he had disappointed his father. Again. Not only was he a shrimp, but he had been the cause of his father's smashed violin. And now this. There was no way he could ever be like his big brother, Leo.

"I'm sure I can find a good job, Papa. A really good one. You'll see. I'll go down to the mill this afternoon."

They were walking along the tracks near the bushes. Papa put his hand out to stop Luc, and they looked down. At the edge of the bushes were several large round animal droppings.

"What's that?" Luc asked.

Papa poked at one mound with a stick. "From a bear, I'd say. And not so old. This is really the Wild West out here. But maybe we'd better not mention wild animals to the women. It might make them too nervous to know there are bears and cougars and even wolves and coyotes in these woods."

Luc stared into the thick forest. Bears? Wolves? He shivered.

When they reached the boxcar, Maman was at the firepit stirring a big, steaming pot, and Madame Poirier was washing and cutting up carrots to add to the soup. The rain had stopped, so everyone was out of the boxcar and around the smoky firepit.

"Smells delicious." Papa sniffed the steaming broth. "Onions, carrots. Where did you get all the fresh vegetables?"

"The man from the laundry has a garden," Maman said. "He brought us a sack of beans, onions, potatoes, and carrots. All good for a soup."

"Was his name Lum King?" Luc asked.

Maman nodded. "He said he knew you from last night."

"Lum King?" Madame Leblanc asked. "What sort of name is that?"

"He's Chinese and very friendly," Luc said. "He wants to learn how to speak more English."

"Humph!" Madame Leblanc sniffed. "We certainly won't be eating food provided by any dirty heathen."

"Lum King's vegetables have made a very good soup for us," Maman said. "Are you sure you wouldn't like to try some?"

"Certainly not." Madame Leblanc glared at her disdainfully and daintily picked at some sardines from a can instead.

When Luc noticed that Louisa was sitting on "his" stump, he stood beside Papa. A cool wind was blowing up from the river, so the warmth from the fire was comforting. After Louisa turned her nose up at Maman's soup, as well, Luc shook his head and wondered how people could be so ignorant.

Maman passed around mugs of soup to the others. "How did it go with the horses this morning?"

"They're magnificent animals." Papa's eyes shone as he rubbed his hands together. "Twenty-nine pairs and a few singles. Mostly big, strong Clydesdales. The best for hauling work. But Luc will have to find another job."

"Why is that?" Maman asked.

Papa shook his head. "He doesn't have the touch, I guess."

Luc kicked at a rock at the edge of the fire and hung his head. "I'll get some other job," he told them, his voice husky. "A good job down at the mill. You'll see."

Papa shrugged. "You could ask, but don't get your hopes up."

Rita piped up. "Then can I go to the stables and help you with the horses, Papa, please? I can do it. I know I can. I'd love a chance to work with horses."

Papa sighed and looked at Maman. She nodded.

Before Papa could say yes, Rita yelled, "Yippee! Can I start right now?"

"At least wait until we've finished our soup, *ma fille*. That will be soon enough. I'll ask Walter Toban, see what he says about a girl working in the stables. He might not like it."

Luc burrowed even farther into his coat. Maman handed him his mug of soup. It was warm in his hands and tasted good and salty, but he had a hard time swallowing it.

After lunch Madame Poirier put a lid on the soup pot and pulled it to the edge of the fire where it would keep warm for later. Maman put Clara and Joseph down for their naps in the boxcar on their beds of cedar boughs and blankets where she would have a nap herself to keep them company. With the fringe of her long plaid scarf swaying, Rita skipped away with Papa as he returned to the stables. Meanwhile the three little Poirier boys explored the bushes around the camp.

"Now don't you boys go far," their mother warned them. "A bear or a wild cougar might get you. Remember, this is the Wild West."

Luc recalled the bear droppings he and Papa had seen on their way back from the stable. Papa had said not to tell the women, that they would worry. Luc peered into the nearby woods. As long as they kept a good fire burning like Tom Sawyer and Huck Finn had on their camping trip, probably no wild animals would approach the boxcar. He added a big log to the fire so it would burn on its own for a while.

The two Leblanc girls were sitting beside the firepit watching him. "Bravo!" Louisa cried. Then she and Isabella applauded him.

Luc grabbed the water pails. "Hey, you three!" he called to the Poirier boys. "You want to go and get some water? I'll show you where we get it." He would leave the two Leblanc sisters there and maybe, if he was lucky, some wild animal would come and grab them both and drag them off for their supper.

As he led the three little fellows away, each swinging an empty water pail, he felt a bit like the Pied Piper. He made them stop and look both ways for trains before crossing the tracks.

Luc planned that after getting the water he would go down to the mill to ask for that job. There must be something at the mill he could do. Piling lumber or sweeping out sawdust. He was sure he could do that.

He tried to hurry back from the laundry to the boxcar with the heavy buckets, but water sloshed out, soaking his stockings. He shouldn't have filled the buckets so much when Lum King had shown them the pump behind the laundry room. It was bad enough that his foot was wet where his sole had a hole. Now both stockings were soaked, as well. The metal handles of the buckets dug into his hands. He stopped to rest for a moment beside the train station. The Poirier boys scurried ahead to the boxcar with their half-filled buckets.

Dan Rogers was there beside the station with a half-dozen young men who had come on the train from Quebec with Luc and his family. Papa's big friend, Le Gros, was there, too. They all had axes, and one fellow had a long two-man saw over his shoulder.

Mr. Rogers explained in a loud voice, "Look, we need all you men at the chainsaws this afternoon to help saw the logs into boards and get the lumber loaded onto that boat down there at the dock. It's a rush job."

The men stared at one another and shrugged. They mumbled and shifted their axes uneasily.

"No understand so much *l'anglais*," Le Gros said in a heavy voice, shaking his shaggy head.

The other men shook their heads, too. "Tree? Chop da tree?" one asked, swinging his axe. "We, um, go now? You show?"

"No, no. Not cutting the trees," Mr. Rogers said, raising his voice. "I need you all to work at the mill. And if you get the job done before the end of the week, there will be a bonus for you."

But the men shrugged some more.

"Eh, Le Gros," Luc said, then explained in French to the big man and his buddies that Mr. Rogers needed them all down at the mill for a special job.

"Ah!" one said. "*Bien sûr!* But how much is the pay?" Luc asked Mr. Rogers.

"Same as the loggers," the manager said. "Two and

a half dollars a day for a ten-hour day. But tell them to report at the mill right now. We're already way behind schedule."

When Luc told the lumberjacks, Le Gros said, "Two and a half dollars a day even down at the mill, eh? That's good. Very good." The other lumberjacks agreed.

"You can tell them to ask for Mr. Johnson, the foreman," Mr. Rogers said. "He'll show them what to do."

Luc told the loggers, and they nodded and shook Mr. Rogers's hand, then Luc's hand. "*Merci*, t'ank you." They grinned and started leaving for the mill.

Mr. Rogers turned to Luc. "Thanks for your help, boy. What's your name again?"

"I'm Luc Godin, sir. And I would like a job, too. Could I go and work in the mill with those men?"

Mr. Rogers shook his head sadly. "Sorry, Luc. You're too young. What are you? Eleven? Twelve?"

"I'm thirteen, almost fourteen." Luc stood as tall as he could and pushed out his chest. "I'm strong. You'll see. I could sweep the floor. Or pile up the lumber maybe?"

"Thirteen, eh? You're André Godin's boy, aren't you? Weren't you going to help your father with the horses? Be a stableboy?"

"No, um, no. Walter Toban said no. He didn't need me, after all."

Before Luc had a chance to ask if there was another job for him, two other young men arrived with their axes. They were big fellows, friends of his older brother, Leo, back in Pointe-Gatineau. Jean-Louis and Zeph. "*Bonjour, Luc. Ça va?*"

"*Bonjour*," he said, nodding to them.

Then they stood beside Mr. Rogers, embarrassingly quiet.

"What's happening?" Luc asked them in French.

"We don't know where to report for work," Jean-Louis said. "Could you ask the boss? You speak the English."

"Jean-Louis and Zeph here want to know where they should go for work," Luc told Mr. Rogers.

"Tell them to go down to the mill, too. Ask for Mr. Johnson. He's got plenty of work for them. And the other men can explain the details."

After Luc told Jean-Louis and Zeph to go to the mill and they left, Mr. Rogers said, "You know, Luc. I just had a thought. I could use a bright fellow like you in the office to translate for me. There are all these new workers coming from Quebec and a lot of them don't speak any English at all. I don't suppose you can read and write in French, too?"

"Of course."

"And what about English?"

"Pretty good. I came first in my English class last year."

Mr. Rogers stroked his chin. "How about coming to work in my office, say, three or four days a week? I could pay you a dollar a day. You'd do some letter writing and help keep the place clean. But, mainly, you'd translate for these new workers. And maybe you could help my son with his mathematics, as well. He's having a hard time."

"Really?" Luc felt like dancing a jig right there in front of the station. Instead he grinned broadly. "I'd love to, sir. When do I start?"

"Today. Yes. You could begin today. I'll meet you at my office in an hour or so and show you around. It's in that big white house up on Pitt River Road."

"Yes, sir!" Luc grabbed the buckets of water and raced back to the boxcar to tell Maman.

Funny, now his water buckets were as light as air.

7

Meeting the Delectable Ruth Victoria

Yippee! Luc had a job! A real job! And three or four days a week at a dollar a day would be three or four dollars a week. Two dollars for Maman and two for him. It wouldn't be long before he saved some money, and he knew exactly what he'd buy with it.

When he got back to the boxcar, Maman was sitting on a stump beside the campfire with Madame Poirier. They both had darning in their laps.

"Guess what, Maman! You'll never guess. I have a job! A real job!" Luc sloshed the water in the buckets as he dropped them beside the campfire and danced around

"*Non, vraiment?* A job? For you?"

"Yes, really! And I start this afternoon. Mr. Rogers said to go to the office in an hour or so, and I'll help with the mail, sweep out the office, and do some translating. And also help his son with his studies."

"And he'll pay you for that?"

"Yes. A dollar a day, three, maybe four days a week. I could give you half and save the rest."

"That's wonderful, my son. I'm proud of you. But you must get cleaned up to work in a fancy office."

In the boxcar Maman rummaged through their clothes quietly because Joseph and Clara were still napping. She pulled Luc's Sunday pants and shirt out of a carpet bag and brushed them, trying to shake out the wrinkles. "And you better clean those boots," she whispered. "Here, take some of this grease."

Luc rubbed thick grease into his boots until the tops were shiny and black. Good thing the hole in the sole didn't show. He put some grease into his dark curly hair, as well, parting it carefully in the middle and brushing it down on the sides. Then he ducked behind the blanket partition and pulled off his everyday shirt, sweater, and breeches. He washed his face and arms with the damp towel Maman had given him. Then he pulled on his last clean pair of stockings and his dark blue woollen pants that he seemed to have had for ages and still hadn't outgrown. They were held up with a pair of suspenders over his good shirt, a pale blue cotton one. It was quite wrinkled, so he tried to smooth down the front. He didn't have any other jacket, so his everyday woollen tweed coat would have to do. He gave his boots one last shine and came out from behind the partition.

"Now don't you look respectable," Madame Poirier said.

"Like a real gentleman." Maman brushed some lint off his coat. "*Bonne chance, mon fils!*"

Louisa was sitting at the other side of the boxcar reading with her sister. She pointed at him and whispered in her sister's ear. They both wiggled their eyebrows at him and giggled.

Luc knew they were laughing at him, but he didn't care. He had a job. A real job! He pulled his cap on at a rakish angle over his right eyebrow, vaulted out of the boxcar, and hurried off to the office.

Not far from the train station, the office was in a tall white house with green trim up on Pitt River Road, as Mr. Rogers had told him. It looked as if the office took up the whole main floor of the house, and the family lived in the upper two stories.

Luc took a deep breath and held it as he knocked on the door under the white sign on which was printed OFFICE in neat black letters. There was a glass window in the door, but it was so dusty he couldn't see through it.

No one came to the door. Luc knocked again. Still no answer, so he pushed it open and blinked. It took a few moments for his eyes to adjust to the dull light. He was in a large gloomy room. There were piles of papers and books everywhere, crowding the bookshelves and tables. Even the dusty windowsills were stacked with books.

A man sat at a heavy wooden desk, hunched over a pile of papers, frowning at them through spectacles. He had a fringe of long grey hair and a sparse grey beard. He didn't look up as Luc entered.

Luc hesitated. He was about to ask for Mr. Rogers when the man came bustling into the room from the door opposite.

"Ah, there you are, my boy," the manager called out. "And you've met Mr. Steely? Steely, this is Luc Godin. He'll be helping us here in the office, mostly with those new men from Quebec. Since he speaks French, and English, as well, he can translate for us."

Mr. Steely looked up then and removed his spectacles. He blinked and stared at Luc with bright blue eyes. "Good." His voice was surprisingly high and wispy. "We need help with all you new Frenchies."

"Benjamin," Mr. Rogers said, "come here, son."

A gangling youth with a mass of blond hair left his desk, which was in a dark corner at the back of the office.

"Luc, this is my son, Benjamin. I hope you'll help him with his studies. I think he spends most of the afternoon staring out the window and dreaming instead of getting the job done." He gave Ben's hair an affectionate tug, and the boy grinned up at him.

"Yes, sir," Luc said. "I'll be happy to do that." He wasn't sure, but he thought Ben was one of the boys who had ridden their bicycles past the train station the day before.

Mr. Rogers put on his hat. "First, though, how about giving this office a good sweeping? Just be sure not to disturb Mr. Steely's piles of papers and ruin his system. You go back to your work, Benjamin. Luc can give you a hand with it after he's finished sweeping. I'm on my way down to the mill now to check on those new fellows. I'll see you later."

There was a broom leaning in a corner, so Luc picked it up and started sweeping with big, vigorous strokes. He would show his new boss what an excellent worker he was, making sure the manager didn't regret hiring him.

"Hold on there, Frenchie!" Mr. Steely coughed into a big white handkerchief. "Not so much dust, if you don't mind."

Luc swept a little less energetically and soon had the dark board floor clear of litter.

Ben threw down his pencil. "I hate this!"

"What is it?" Luc asked. "Maybe I can help."

"This stupid spelling. I have to learn all these words for the test by the end of the week." He shook a paper at Luc, showing him a long list.

"*Zoo-eee!* Must be a hundred words there!"

"It *is* a hundred. I just can't concentrate to learn them." Ben rattled the paper. "There are too many."

Luc looked closer. Two columns of words filled the page. Most of the words were easy ones he had learned years ago. "I bet you already know how to spell a lot of these. How about I ask you to spell them? All the words you already know, we can cross off the list. Then we can concentrate on the words you don't know."

It turned out that Ben knew how to spell more than half.

"See. You only have thirty-eight to learn."

"Better than a hundred, I guess."

Luc showed Ben how to write each word three times, studying every letter hard. He had discovered that trick years ago when he first began learning English.

After they worked for a while, Ben threw down his pencil again. "I need a break. How about going out to get some fresh air?"

"Won't your father mind?"

"Ha! This is the most work I've done for a long time."

"Well, if you're sure." Luc followed Ben outside. As they slipped by Mr. Steely's desk, he didn't even glance up from his thick ledger.

"How come you're not at school today?" Luc asked Ben.

"I go in the morning shift, eight to noon. The little guys in grades one to four go in the afternoon, and the rest of us go in the morning. What about you? Aren't you going to school?"

"I don't think so. Not right away, anyway. We can't really afford it right now. I already finished grade eight last June. I'd sure like to finish high school, though."

"What? You actually like going to school?"

Luc nodded. "I always wanted to be a doctor when I grew up. Even when I was a little kid."

"There's a college in New Westminster where you can take high school. It's a boarding school but has day students, too. That's where I'll be going in a couple of years, because Millside School out here goes only to grade eight. Good thing I've already got a good bicycle to get me to school in town. Want to see it?"

"Your bicycle? I'd love to!"

The bicycle was leaning against the wall beside the back door, all glossy black except for the handlebars and the spokes in the big wheels, which glistened silver. There was an oily chain running from a sprocket in the centre of the back wheel to a chain ring that was attached to the pedals.

"*Magnifique!* It's the swellest thing I've ever seen." Luc stroked the thick leather seat. "How does it work?"

"You push down on these pedals like this, and it moves this chain, which makes the back wheel turn."

"How do you stop?"

"You pedal backwards. It doesn't always work, so sometimes you have to drag your feet. I got it for my birthday when I turned eleven in the summer. My father had it sent up special from Seattle in the United States. Ever ridden a wheel before?"

"Never, but I sure would love to try."

"Go on. It's not so hard once you get used to it." Ben rolled the bicycle to the tree-lined driveway that went along the side of the house and down to some wooden stables at the back of their garden. "I can hold the bicycle up in the back here until you get on."

Luc gripped the handlebars and swung one leg over the seat. He wasn't sure what to do next.

"Just sit up on the seat and put your feet on the pedals," Ben told him.

Luc tried to, but the bicycle was surprisingly tipsy. "How do you make it stay upright?"

"Bicycles won't stay up unless they're moving. I can hold you, if you like. You push the pedals with your feet."

Luc pressed down on the right pedal. The bicycle lurched forward.

"I'm holding you back here!" Ben shouted, running behind him. "Don't worry!"

Eventually, after a few crashes, Luc was able to stay upright. He coasted along the gravel driveway to the stable and pumped back up through the grassy garden. Ben jogged beside him, yelling encouragement.

Luc's heart beat fast. He was sweating with effort as he pedalled hard. He marvelled that the more he pushed down on the pedals, the faster he went. Soon he was flying around the backyard, panting, the wind on his face and in his hair. Glorious!

As he pumped up the leaf-strewn driveway toward the house, he glanced up. Someone was coming out the back door. She was tall and slender with long blond hair flowing over the shoulders of a light-coloured dress. The girl looked at him and smiled, and his pounding heart swelled. He had never in his whole life seen such a lovely vision.

The bicycle wobbled, and Luc crashed into a prickly shrub.

"Oh, my goodness!" the girl exclaimed, covering her cheeks with her hands.

Luc's feet were tangled in the pedals, but he scrambled up, brushing off leaves and twigs and feeling his face flush.

"And who's this trying to ride your bicycle, Ben?" The girl's voice was light and sweet, but Luc thought he could detect a gentle note of mockery.

Ben ran to help him lift the bicycle. "This is Luc. He arrived with his family on the train yesterday."

"Ah, one of the newcomers from Quebec."

"How do you do?" Luc stammered, rubbing his chin where it had hit the handlebars. At least she hadn't called him "Frenchie."

"This is my sister, Ruth," Ben said.

"Are you hurt?" Ruth's blue eyes seemed concerned.

"Hurt? Me? Oh, no. I'm fine. Just fine." Her eyes were so piercingly blue that Luc couldn't think of anything else to say. His heart was thumping madly.

A small black dog scooted out of the house.

"Oh, Scottie!" She gathered the little dog up in her arms and peered up at Luc over her pet. "This is my naughty, naughty Scottie," she said, laughing. "He's so restless that he needs a walk every morning, noon, and night. Don't you, boy?"

"He's cute." Luc patted the dog's wiry fur.

Yipping, the dog licked his hand and wagged its stubby tail.

"Oooh," Ruth murmured, "I do think my Scottie has made a new friend." She smiled a dimpled smile at Luc, and he felt himself blush. She even smelled lovely, like flowers, or soap or …

"Well, we're off to the general store to get some apples for Mother to make a pie for dinner." She clipped a leash to Scottie's neck and sashayed away.

Luc stared at the gate long after she was gone.

"Um, want to try the bicycle again?" Ben asked. "I think you almost got it that time."

"Try the bicycle?" Luc shook his head to clear it. "Sure thing." As he mounted the bicycle, the gate opened.

It must be Ruth returning, Luc thought. He caught his breath.

But it was Dan Rogers. "What are you two doing out here? Luc, I'm paying you to tutor Benjamin. And, Ben, you have to study for that spelling examination."

"Yes, of course, sir." Luc leaned the bicycle against the house and led Ben back into the dim office.

* * *

For the rest of the week Luc worked at the office. Most of the time he was sweeping and putting books on the shelves. As long as he stayed out of Mr. Steely's way, the old man didn't complain.

Luc translated a few letters that came from Quebec from French to English. They were pretty easy, since he had his trusty French-English dictionary for the really hard words.

He even cleaned the windows when Ben was away at school in the mornings. Sometimes in the afternoons he helped Ben with his studies, mostly mathematics but English and science, as well. When they had a break, Luc practised riding Ben's bicycle around the backyard and hoped for another glimpse of Ruth. Even her name was beautiful, he thought: Ruth Victoria Rogers. If he were a songwriter, he would have written a tune for her.

Dan Rogers needed him several times a day to help interpret when the workers from Quebec came in and had questions about work or their living quarters.

"Don't know how we could have ever managed without your help, Luc," Mr. Rogers said at the end of the week, giving him a narrow brown envelope with four one-dollar bills inside. "On top of your help as a translator, I hear that Ben got an A in his spelling test for the first time this year."

"Thank you, sir."

Luc ran all the way back to the boxcar in the gathering gloom of the evening. "Maman!" he shouted, waving the envelope. "Look!"

She was at the campfire with Madame Poirier, stirring a stew in a big pot for their supper. "Well done, Luc," she said, smiling. "I'm very proud of you. Put it away in a safe place now."

"Here's two dollars for you, Maman."

"Thank you. It'll help buy something special for our Sunday dinner."

Luc found an empty tobacco tin. He folded his two one-dollar bills, dropped them into the tin, and screwed on the lid securely. "It won't be long," he told himself, stashing the tin under his makeshift bed in the boxcar. "It won't be long before I have enough money to buy that bicycle. My very own bicycle!"

8

Trek to the Royal City

One Sunday evening, after they had been in the boxcar for a couple of weeks, the families were all around the campfire after a supper of chicken stew and store-bought bread. Luc was leaning against the boxcar, sitting on a stump, and reading *The Adventures of Tom Sawyer.* It was the fourth time he had read the book, and though it was just as exciting and funny as the first time, he longed for something new to read.

"I can't believe our houses still aren't ready," Madame Leblanc complained, shaking out her long skirt. "I simply can't stand this place another day. My girls and I have run out of clean clothes, and that general store has only the bare necessities. Also, we haven't had our hair done for weeks since we left Quebec. We must go to the city tomorrow."

"Do you mean all the way to New Westminster?" Maman asked.

Madame Leblanc nodded. "Yes, of course, my dear."

"But how will you get there, Thérèse?" Madame Boileau asked.

"We can take the morning train. I saw the schedule

at the station. We can leave here at 10:30, so we'll be in the city before noon in time to have a lovely luncheon at the tea room at Eaton's. And the evening train leaves New Westminster at 4:00, so that should be plenty of time to get our hair done." She fluffed out her light brown curls. "You must all come."

Madame Poirier laughed. "I don't think I could bring along my three little hoodlums to a fancy tea room. No, you go and buy us a nice treat and I'll stay here and keep the home fires burning. I'll even look after your little Joseph for you, Josephine, if you want to go."

Maman was sitting behind Rita, braiding her long dark hair. She smiled dreamily. "It would be fun to see the city. I wonder if New Westminster is like Montreal. I heard they call it the Royal City because the queen in England loved it so much. I haven't been to a city for years. But I think I'd better stay home. Maybe I could go next time."

Madame Leblanc pursed her lips. "Too bad. You know we can't really go without a man to carry our parcels. And, most important, to help us with the English. So I wonder if ..."

All the women turned and stared at Luc.

"Oh, no," he groaned loudly, hiding his face behind his book. The idea of sitting around a fancy tea room with Madame Leblanc and her conceited daughters didn't appeal to him one bit.

Louisa and Isabella giggled at him, as usual.

"I heard there's a big public library in the city where people can borrow books," Maman coaxed him. "You could find something new to read there."

"And, of course, I would pay for your train fare," Madame Leblanc said.

Luc couldn't think of an excuse. Madame Leblanc knew he didn't have to work at the office on Mondays.

Maybe he could get a good book to read at the public library. For that he would have to endure a day with Madame Leblanc, Madame Boileau, and their daughters.

The next morning was overcast, with a frigid wind whistling up from the river. The whole boxcar was a-twitter with mothers and their daughters getting ready to go on a rare shopping expedition to the city of New Westminster, primping, patting, and perfuming one another.

"But you can't wear those dirty old breeches to the city, Luc," Maman said. "Put on your Sunday pants."

Across the other side of the boxcar, Louisa and Isabella sniggered at him. How he hated those girls!

"Too bad I have to work at the stables today so I can't go, too," Rita said, laughing at him. She loved working with the horses, and Walter Toban had said that she was one of the finest stable*boys* he had. "Ta-ta now." She pulled on her plaid scarf and waved to him on her way out with Papa. "Have fun now."

He stuck his tongue out at her, and Louisa and Isabella laughed even harder.

By ten o'clock they were flouncing across the tracks, all dressed in their Sunday best. Madame Leblanc led the way with a daughter on each arm. She wore her Sunday hat decorated with plumes and artificial fruit. Behind her tottered Madame Boileau on high heels, with her two silent daughters, Martha and Bertha, wearing matching red coats and hats. Luc brought up the rear, shuffling after the perfumed cloud.

The women gave him the money to buy the tickets, seven return fares to New Westminster.

The station master raised his eyebrows. "Aha! Taking all the lovely ladies out for a special day in the big bad city, I see."

Luc nodded. "Um, yes."

The station master laughed. "Well, now, don't let them lead a fine young man like you astray."

Luc was glad the women didn't understand much English.

Madame Leblanc led the way into the train. "These look like the best seats." She and Madame Boileau sat on two long wooden seats facing each other, with a daughter on either side.

Luc found a seat as far away from them as possible. He had a long bench to himself, but before the train left the station, Louisa and Isabella switched seats. They plunked themselves down beside him. He slid over, but Louisa sidled closer, so he moved until he was squashed against the side, with his face pressed against the window. The sisters poked each other and giggled excitedly. He tried to ignore them and concentrate on peering out the window as the train left Fraser Mills. It was hard to do with Louisa breathing heavily in his ear.

The train followed the Fraser River, which was lined with tangles of willow bushes growing on its sandy banks. Bare branches waved as the train chugged by. As it approached the city, it went under a two-storey bridge that spanned the river. At the edge of the waterfront were several big grey stone buildings and many haphazard-looking wooden sheds. Finally, the train shunted to a stop at the New Westminster station.

Isabella plucked at Luc's back. "Come on now. This is where we have to get out, or we'll end up going all the way to Vancouver."

For a second Luc thought about how great it would be to get away from them. But the girls dragged him into the aisle and he had to follow them and their mother out of the train. The station was the biggest building he had ever been in. He felt dwarfed by the high ceilings and huge windows.

"I'm feeling a little peckish. Aren't you?" Madame Leblanc said as she led the parade across the shiny marble floor, through the train station, and outside to the street. "I think we should have our luncheon in the tea room at Eaton's first before we do our shopping."

Madame Boileau agreed. "But how do we know where Eaton's is?"

"That looks like it down there on the main street. And just look at all these wonderful people!" Madame Leblanc exclaimed, hooking her arm into Madame Boileau's. Their daughters toddled after them, and the crowd on the busy boardwalk parted as they sailed toward the big department store.

Luc had seldom been to such a big city. Pointe-Gatineau, in comparison, was a village with dirt roads and no boardwalks. Everywhere he looked there were people: old ones, youngsters, all ages. Mobs strolled along the crowded boardwalk or rode by in horse-drawn buggies on the cobblestone road. There were even a few people riding bicycles, mostly safety bicycles like Ben's, with the two wheels the same size. But, as well, there were a few high-wheelers, or penny farthings, as they were called sometimes. They had two wheels, too, but the back one was tiny and the front one was as tall as Luc and had the pedals attached directly to it. Now that really looked like fun.

And there was even an occasional automobile!

Madame Leblanc stopped abruptly in front of a shop. ROSE'S FINE LADIES' WEAR declared the sign in the big window. "Oh, my! Such beautiful undergarments! Gorgeous, gorgeous! I simply must get some of those for my daughters! And maybe even some for me, too." She giggled. "Come inside, everyone." She swept the girls into the shop. "Don't just stand there, Luc," she said, tugging at his sleeve. "We might need you here."

Once in the lingerie shop, Luc didn't know where to look or where to stand to be inconspicuous. Lining the packed shop were mannequins of women with very large bosoms, dressed in the most revealing underclothing with frills, ribbons, and lace. Luc tried to keep his eyes on the dark brown oiled wooden floor. His face burned with embarrassment. He was sure Louisa was laughing at him. Probably everyone was.

Finally, he mumbled, "I'll wait outside," and he hurried back out where he breathed a sigh of relief. But the sidewalk beside the shop was still teeming with people, and the crowd pushed him along until he came to a large brick structure, the Carnegie Building. A sign over the door made him stop: FREE PUBLIC LIBRARY. OPEN 10:00 A.M. TO 10:00 P.M., MONDAY TO FRIDAY.

He ducked out of the mob and into the building. As he entered a shadowy room, the most wonderful smell met him. The smell of books. Hundreds and hundreds of books. Maybe even thousands of books. Never in his life had he seen so many. All the walls of the large room were covered with rows and rows of books from the floor to shelves so high you would need a ladder to reach them. Luc couldn't imagine so many wonderful stories.

Directly in front of the entrance was a tall, round desk. A young woman wearing glasses stood behind it. LIBRARIAN, the sign in front of her declared.

"Hello, may I help you?" She smiled down at Luc in a friendly way.

"It, um, it says free library." He hesitated. "Does that mean people can borrow books for free?"

"Why, yes, it does. All you need is a library card."

"Oh." So there was a catch. Of course, he didn't have a library card. And no money to buy one. "Maybe I could just look at your books then?"

She laughed. "I think you must be a READER." The way she said "READER" was as if it was all in capitals. "What's your favourite book?"

"I like *The Adventures of Tom Sawyer.*"

"That's a good story. Have you read *The Adventures of Huckleberry Finn*? It's by Mark Twain, as well."

He shook his head. "No. Just *Tom Sawyer*."

"You could borrow *Huckleberry Finn*, if you like. I think you'd find it even more exciting. I'm sure we have a copy." She left her perch. A few moments later she returned with the book and thrust it into his hands. It was big and thick and heavy, and was, Luc was sure, filled with all kinds of marvellous adventures.

"But I don't have a library card for your library. And I don't have any money to buy one."

The librarian laughed. "Our library cards are free. You just fill out this form, then you can borrow books from our library anytime. We do have a few rules, though. You may take out two books at a time and keep them for three weeks. And you must always wash your hands before you read any of our books."

The librarian gave him a form to fill out and a straight pen and a small bottle of ink. His name was easy. Luc Godin. For address he wrote Fraser Mills townsite. He didn't mention the boxcar. He had to leave the name of his school blank. Where it said "signature" he signed his name with a flourish.

"No school?" she asked him after he blotted the form on a blotting paper and gave it back.

"Not this year."

"I found another book you'll enjoy." She showed him a copy of *Treasure Island.*

He flipped through it and saw that it was about pirates and buried treasure. "This looks like the best book ever."

The librarian smiled and stamped the books. "Welcome to the New Westminster Public Library, Luc."

He left the library clutching the books to his chest. He couldn't wait to get back to the boxcar to read them.

"There he is, Maman!" Louisa shrieked. "Coming out of that building!"

Before he could duck back into the safety of the library, Louisa and Isabella pounced on him and dragged him to their mother.

"Now wherever did you get to, young man?" she demanded. "Where were you when we needed you? We can't buy a single thing if you aren't there to help us with the English, now can we?"

There was no escape. He would have to accompany the ladies around the city for the rest of the day. But at least he had his books to look forward to.

Soon his arms were so piled up with bags and parcels tied with string that he couldn't see where he was going. There was even a large sack of ripe tomatoes that Madame Leblanc had insisted on buying. "All these lovely tomatoes!" she had cried. "Such a bargain!"

Louisa and Isabella had to keep plucking at Luc's sleeves to guide him through the throng of shoppers. Finally, it was almost four o'clock and time to catch the train home.

"Hurry, hurry!" Madame Leblanc panted as she ushered them down the boardwalk and across the cobblestone road to the train station. They were all wearing new outfits, except Luc, of course. Madame Leblanc's outfit was a froth of frills and lace and petticoats. And she also had a new hat with a broad brim decorated with a spray of flowers.

Although the train was already there, she stopped to admire herself in the full-length mirror beside the door. Then, clutching her new hat, she led the way up the steps and inside the train. "These look like the best seats. We'll sit here. Now get our tickets ready for the conductor, Luc," she directed.

Luc dumped all the parcels on a seat to search through his pockets for the tickets.

Madame Leblanc spread her wide, frilly skirt and sat down. There was a loud squirting sound, and a look of alarm flashed across her face. "*Eh, mon dieu!*" she squealed, leaping to her feet. The back of her new skirt was dripping. She had sat on her big bag of ripe tomatoes!

9

The Bicycle Disaster

A few weeks later their houses still weren't ready, so the four families continued to live in the boxcar. Sometimes there was a bleakness to Maman's thin face when she stared out at the dark woods. Luc thought that was when she must be remembering their old house, the neat cottage in Pointe-Gatineau on the banks of the river. That was where they had buried Leo in the churchyard, and where they would return one day to visit his grave.

One Saturday morning only the Poiriers and Godins were sitting around the campfire. The Boileaus and the Leblancs had gone to the general store for supplies. Madame Leblanc was still refusing to accept the delicious fruits and vegetables that Lum King brought them regularly. She insisted that her family eat only store-bought food, so they lived mostly on cans of beans and sardines.

A flock of agitated crows cawed in the branches of the big maple tree as it filtered the early-morning sunshine. Luc sat on his stump, bouncing his little brother on his knee. The little boy giggled.

Although it was Saturday, Papa wanted to go to the stables to check on the horses because the old granddaddy, Thunder, was sick.

"Want me to come, too?" Rita asked.

"Maybe you should. You have a special touch with those animals, especially old Thunder. He's taken a shine to you."

He didn't mention how useless Luc had been with the horses, but Luc knew that was what he was thinking.

"Will we see you at noon then?" Maman asked Papa.

"Yes. See you then." He left with Rita skipping at his side, her long braid swinging from side to side.

"Just look at this sunshine," Maman said. "After all that rain, it's certainly a welcome sight. I can't believe it's already almost November with this warm weather. Back home in Quebec I'm sure the snow has started already."

"For a while there I thought it would never stop raining," Madame Poirier said.

Luc pulled off his sweater.

"Luc," Maman said, "that shirt's filthy. How did it ever get so dirty?"

He glanced down. The front of his shirt was blotched with soup stains and ashes from clearing out the firepit. He tried to scrape off the worst of the dirt with his fingernails, but it didn't work.

"I must do something about washing our clothes so we'll have something clean to wear for Sunday Mass tomorrow," Maman said. "Maybe I could take them to the laundry, and if I wash them myself, Lum King won't charge me too much. But someone will have to look after the little ones."

"Clara can stay with us," Madame Poirier offered. "She can bring her dolls, and I'll watch her."

"*Merci,*" Maman said. "Luc, could you mind Joseph for the morning?"

"Sure. Mr. Rogers doesn't need me on the weekends."

Maman gathered up their clothes, including Luc's shirt, into a big bundle. Then she lifted the bundle to her shoulder and left.

Luc sat Joseph on the stump and quickly pulled his sweater back on. It was scratchy against his bare skin, but it wasn't warm enough to go around with no shirt on. Besides, he didn't want Louisa to see his puny arms. He knew she and her sister would laugh at him.

Joseph was fussy. "Maman, Maman," he kept calling.

"How about going for a walk? You can ride up on my shoulders." Luc buttoned up his brother's coat and pulled a woolly hat over his curls. "That should keep you warm enough." He lifted his little brother up onto his shoulders. "Hang on now. We're going for a horsey ride."

Joseph's fat little fingers threaded into Luc's long hair, and he chuckled as Luc jogged along the train tracks, holding on to his little brother's feet in their soft leather boots. They went past the train station, the general store, and the laundry. Luc got tired of jogging, so he slowed to a bouncy gallop, and Joseph giggled harder. Soon they had left the small settlement of mill buildings and houses and there was nothing but bush on both sides of the tracks.

At the sound of tires crunching the cinders, Luc swung around. It was Ben and one of his pals on their bicycles. They skidded to a stop beside him. "Hey, Luc!" Ben called out. "How you doing?"

"Hi, Ben."

"This is Harry." Ben pointed with his thumb to his friend, a tall, cheerful-looking fellow wearing a tweed cap. "Want to come riding with us? We're going along the tracks to Brunette Creek to go fishing."

"Can't," Luc said, nodding at Harry. "No wheels. Besides, I have to look after my brother this morning."

"Tell you what," Ben said. "You ride my bicycle and double your brother, and Harry can double me on his bicycle."

"Sure would like to." Luc lifted his little brother from his shoulders. "Want to go for a bicycle ride, Joey?"

Joseph gurgled at him. Luc propped him up on the seat of Ben's bicycle. Joseph gurgled more and tipped over. Luc caught him before he fell. "I don't think it's going to work. He's too small to hang on."

"Try sitting him on the crossbar," Harry said. "That's how I double my sister sometimes."

"All right. I'll try that." Luc sat Joseph on the crossbar and showed him how to grip the handlebars tight. "That's better." Luc pushed the bicycle forward. "I can keep an eye on him here."

Joseph chuckled with pleasure and kicked out his little feet. He loved riding on the bicycle.

"Hold on tight now," Luc told him as he mounted the bicycle. He pushed off with one foot and started pedalling. At first it was difficult to get his balance, but soon he was gliding along, pushing down on the pedals, trying to catch up to the other boys.

Ben was sitting on the seat of Harry's bike with his legs outstretched, and Harry was standing on the pedals, pumping like mad. The cinder path along the tracks was probably the fastest way to the creek.

"Hey, you guys! Wait up!" Luc pedalled furiously to catch up. "Wait for me!"

"*Wheeee!*" Joseph sang out, swinging his little legs.

The wind blew through Luc's hair. He breathed hard, gulping in the fresh air. The bushes at the side of the tracks were a blur. Yes! Freedom! Speed! This was travelling! One day he would have his own bicycle, and this is how he'd ride. He threw back his head and grinned. This was the best!

He had almost caught up to Harry and Ben when a terrible thing happened.

A log was on the path. Luc jerked the handlebars sharply to avoid it. The bicycle swerved and one of Joseph's little feet got caught in the wheel. He let out a piercing scream, and the bicycle lurched off the path.

Luc lost control, and they tumbled in a heap down the embankment to the spiky grass below. As he fell on top of the baby, Luc scraped his leg and his shin was embedded with cinders, but he didn't feel anything. His ears were filled with the baby's screeches.

"Oh, Joey!" Luc rolled off his brother. Joseph's eyes were squeezed shut and his mouth was wide open, shrieking.

"What is it?" Then Luc saw his brother's foot. It was tangled in the front wheel. He fought frantically to dislodge it from the spokes, but the more he tried, the harder Joseph screamed.

Ben and Harry rushed back. They wheeled down the slope and stopped with a jolt. Ben knelt beside Luc.

"It's his foot!" Luc cried. "It got caught in the spokes!" Finally, he managed to free the baby's foot. His leg wasn't bleeding, but it was twisted at an odd angle.

The little boy screamed and screamed some more. His red cheeks and nose streamed with tears and mucus. Now he wouldn't let Luc even near his leg, pulling away from him.

"We need help," Ben said, ready to take off.

"We can't leave him here alone!" Luc shouted over Joseph's screams. "I'll stay with him. Can you get my mother?"

"Sure thing."

"She's at the laundry. Tell her to come quick." Luc didn't even finish before Ben and Harry took off, their bicycles spraying cinders in their haste.

Luc tried stroking Joseph's back to comfort him, but the baby wouldn't let him. He just screamed more. His nose streamed and his face was blotchy.

It seemed hours before the boys finally arrived with Maman. She came at a run, her long skirts gathered. Lum King jogged beside her, carrying a large laundry basket on his head.

Maman swept the still-screaming toddler into her arms. "*Ah, mon pauvre petit bébé!* What is it?" She was panting hard, and her face was red. Her hair had come out of its usually tidy knot at the back of her neck, and wisps blew into her face.

"It's his leg, Maman. I'm so sorry ..."

Maman shook her head, pushing back her loose hair and rocking the little boy in her arms. "What happened?"

"His leg. It got caught in the wheel ..."

Maman looked mystified.

"I was giving him a ride on Ben's bicycle," Luc attempted to explain. "He really liked it."

Maman tried to examine Joseph's leg, prodding it gently. No matter how carefully she touched it, though, Joseph screamed and pulled it away.

Lum King knelt beside her and studied the leg, too. "Any blood?"

"Blood?" That was an English word Maman didn't know. She shrugged and glanced at Luc.

"No," Luc told him. "I didn't see any blood." He explained the question to Maman in French.

Maman shook her head. "No see blood."

"Baby need doctor," Lum King said. "Doctor now. Leg not look so good. Maybe, um ..." He struggled to find the right word, then picked up a twig and snapped it.

"You think his leg might be broken?" Luc asked.

Lum King nodded. "Broke. Yes, leg broke."

Maman wrapped Joseph in her shawl tenderly, and he snuggled into her arms, still sobbing.

"Is there a doctor in the townsite?" Luc asked. "Can we take him there?"

Lum King shook his head. "No doctor here in mill town on Saturday. You take baby to doctor in town. Sapperton. Dr. Scott. His office beside post office. Velly good doctor. He look after baby."

Maman didn't understand.

"We have to take Joseph to the doctor in Sapperton," Luc explained in French.

"We not have cart," she told Lum King. "Or horse. How baby go to doctor?"

"I'll go and tell Papa," Luc said. "There must be a cart and horse around the stables that we can use."

"Yes. You go to stable velly fast for horse and cart," Lum King said. "Doctor need see baby now. We take baby to stable in basket. Then leg, we not hurt so much."

Luc rushed away to the stables. How was he ever going to explain this accident to his father? The worst part was that it had happened because of his father's most hated contraption — the bicycle.

And the whole thing was all Luc's fault.

10

Rushing Joseph to the Doctor

The quickest way to the stables was straight south toward the river, then west through the mill yard. Luc sprinted across the marshy fields, trying to avoid the deeper puddles and muckier swamps, but mud splashed up onto his scraped legs, stinging them. Gritting his teeth at the pain, he kept on running, taking a shortcut through the mill yard and dashing around piles of lumber and machinery.

"Hey, kid!" a mill worker yelled at him. "No fooling around the lumber."

Luc didn't stop to explain. He darted away, not stopping until he finally reached the stables. His breath tore at his lungs. He stared down a row of stalls. They were empty. All the big Clydesdale horses were out working, probably hauling logs up in the woods north of the village. Maybe Papa was gone, too.

Luc raced to another row. Someone was at the end, raking straw around an empty stall. Luc swooped down the aisle, his running footsteps echoing on the board floor. It was Rita.

"Where's Papa?" he panted.

"Out back, leaving to take a team up into the woods. What happened? You're all muddy and sweaty."

"What's the quickest way to him? I have to stop him!"

"Why?" she asked.

"It's Joseph. He's hurt. Have to get him … to doctor's."

"Oh, no! What happened?"

"No time to explain."

"If we hurry, we might catch Papa." She dropped her rake and led him racing out the side door and around to the back of the stable.

Papa was there with a stableboy, hitching up a cart behind a pair of big, shiny brown horses.

"Papa!" Luc called. "Wait!"

"Luc! Why are you here? What is it? What's happened?"

Luc explained that there had been an accident.

"But how did it happen?"

Luc was breathing hard. He gulped. His sweater made his sweaty back itch like crazy. He yanked at the neck. "My fault," he said, still gasping for air. "I was giving Joseph … a ride … on Ben's bicycle. And his foot." He gulped hard. "Well, it got caught … in the front wheel."

"Those darn contraptions!" Papa exploded. "Where's he now?"

Luc flinched. "Maman's bringing him here. With Lum King … carrying him in a laundry basket." Luc took a deep breath. "Lum King … he said maybe Joseph's leg's broken. So we have to get him to the doctor in Sapperton right away. They'll be here soon."

"We'll use this cart. You go tell Walter Toban that we have to borrow one of his teams to go to town. He's probably in his office. Rita, show Luc where it is." He turned away to finish hitching the team to the cart.

Luc felt the heat of his father's anger. He wished he could explain that he hadn't meant to hurt his little brother. That it had been a complete accident. But there was nothing he could do now, so he followed Rita. She showed him where the office was at the front of the stables.

"You have to knock," she told him.

Luc knocked, and a gruff voice answered, "Come in."

Mr. Toban was behind a big wooden desk, poring over some books.

"Excuse me, sir," Luc said.

"What is it, boy?" Mr. Toban growled.

"My father said to tell you we have to borrow a wagon and horses to go to town."

"Why's that, boy? We need them up in the woods today."

"There's been an accident and we have to get my brother to the doctor right away."

"Then be off," the old man said, dismissing them.

Papa had finished hitching up the horses to the cart when Maman arrived with Lum King, each holding a side of the laundry basket, trying not to jolt the baby inside. His red cheeks were shiny with tears, and he was tucked in with Maman's shawl. Ben and Harry followed behind on their bicycles.

Lum King explained that it was very important to get the little boy to the doctor in the nearby village of Sapperton as quickly as possible.

Papa nodded and said gruffly, "Yes, yes. Put baby in back."

They bundled the little boy into the back of the cart, still in the basket, but in Maman's arms.

"Thank you, Lum King," Maman said.

Lum King patted Joseph's cheek. "Baby be fine. Dr. Scott, he velly good doctor. He fix baby."

"You better come, too, Luc, to help explain to the doctor," Papa said.

Luc scrambled up beside Papa.

"Rita," Maman said in French, "go and tell Madame Poirier what happened. Ask her to keep Clara until we return."

"And what ever you do," Papa added, "stay away from those dangerous contraptions." He shook his fist and glared at Ben and Harry and their bicycles.

Before Luc had a chance to explain that it wasn't their fault, that he was the one who'd had an accident with Joseph, Papa slapped the reins and shouted, "Gee-yup," to the horses. They trotted away along the corduroy road that led to the main road. Luc was glad his new friends didn't understand French.

Straggly trees and bushes lined both sides of the narrow, muddy road. As the cart bounced from one rut to another, Maman tried to keep Joseph's leg as still as possible. Her forehead was wet with perspiration from the effort. Joseph fretted, but eventually the bouncing lulled him to sleep.

Papa didn't talk to Luc. He just held the reins, stared straight ahead, his thick eyebrows knotted angrily, and directed the big horses as they clomped down the road.

After travelling for about half an hour, they reached Sapperton. The road widened and was a little less bumpy. Houses and shops lined the road, but Sapperton was a village like Pointe-Gatineau — nothing at all like the bustling city of New Westminster.

"Lum King said the doctor's office was on the main street," Luc said. "Just past the post office on the left side."

Papa nodded. He still hadn't talked to Luc about the accident. Luc didn't know what to say, how to explain that he hadn't meant to hurt his little brother.

"There's the post office." Luc pointed at a tall wooden building with a sign on it: ROYAL CANADIAN MAIL.

Papa guided his horses to the edge of the gravel road. "Whoa!" he cried. They stopped in front of a brown house with a small wooden sign over the door: MR. JOHN SCOTT, MD. He jumped out of the cart to tie the horses to a hitching post.

Meanwhile Luc helped Maman lower his little brother in the laundry basket. They carried him to the doctor's office door, but it was locked.

Maman shook her head. "But we must try. Ring the bell. Maybe the doctor's at home."

Luc rang the doorbell. They waited. Maman's brow was creased with worry. Luc rang the doorbell again. He tried to peer through the window, but all was in darkness inside.

"Maybe there's another door," Maman suggested.

"I'll go and see," Luc said. He raced around the house to a narrow back porch, leaped up the steps, and banged on the back door.

"Yes, what is it?" An older woman with a sharp face pulled the door open almost immediately.

"It's my little brother! He's hurt. There's been an accident. We need the doctor."

"He's out visiting patients as usual on Saturdays. Where's your brother now?"

"My mother has him at the front door."

"Why didn't you say so, boy?" The woman abruptly slammed the door in his face.

Luc didn't know what to think. He raced back to the front. There, the woman had opened the front door.

"Come in, madam. Bring your little boy inside." The woman's voice was surprisingly kindly now.

Luc helped Maman carry Joseph as the woman ushered them inside to a small stuffy waiting room that smelled of medicine. There were a few chairs and a big sturdy-looking table.

"Wait here, madam. I'll try to reach the doctor at the hospital by our telephone and tell him you're here."

"Thank you," Maman murmured, gently placing Joseph on the table. He was still asleep in the basket.

Luc brought a chair closer to the table for her.

Maman sat down gratefully and gave him a little smile. She brushed the curly hair from Joseph's brow, frowning worriedly at him. His eyelids fluttered.

"I'm really sorry, Maman," Luc started to say.

"I know you are, Luc. You would never hurt Joseph on purpose. But I think what your father feels about those bicycles is true. They're dangerous machines."

Luc nodded. But he remembered that giddy instant of feeling weightless and free when they were gliding along the train tracks. Glorious! He couldn't tell Maman about it, though, not after what had happened.

He looked around the room. There were two faded pictures of trees in heavy frames. The air was warm and close. Luc paced on the worn carpet.

The front doorbell rang, and Papa entered. "You can go out and watch for the doctor until we need you, Luc. And keep an eye on those horses. I don't think they're used to so much traffic."

The air was fresher outside. Luc took a deep breath and went down to the hitching post. The horses were jittery. Muscles the size of Luc's fist in their legs and chests twitched and quivered. They snorted at him.

"It's all right, big horses. It's all right." Luc tried to

sound soothing, but his voice, even to his ears, was nervous and scared. Every time he got near a horse, any horse, he was flooded with the memory of that terrifying spring day a few months ago when he and his brother, Leo, were speeding along on a cart behind two galloping horses, Leo laughing, urging the horses on, faster, faster …

Usually, Luc was able to stop the memory, but this time he couldn't. His head whirled as he felt how the cart had bounced off the road and crashed and they were both thrown between the horses. He couldn't shut out the sound of the thundering hooves, the ground shaking, Leo's screams, and the terrible silence when he lost consciousness.

It was a miracle that Luc had survived practically unhurt. That was what everyone had said. His brother hadn't been so lucky. That day he had died, crushed under the big animals' hooves.

Now even the smell of the horses, their hot, sweaty, salty animal smell, churned Luc's stomach.

Luc swallowed hard and shook his head, trying to clear it. He backed away from the horses, from their smell, and stumbled along the boardwalk. A few people were out strolling, but there was no one who looked like a doctor.

After a last glance at the horses, Luc wandered away, avoiding other horses tied to hitching posts at the road's edge. He passed several small shops, including Martin's, a second-hand shop with a dusty window filled with all sorts of trinkets and household goods. Next to it was a store that caused his heart to lurch, then to beat madly. A bicycle shop! The door was wide open, beckoning.

Luc looked around again. Still no sign of the doctor, so he dashed up the steps and peeked into the shop. A bell tinkled as he entered.

He took a deep breath and inhaled the aroma, a mixture of oil, metal, and leather. Glorious! There were rows of all kinds of bicycles. Long tandem ones for two people, and tall ones like the penny farthings, or high-wheelers, with long, gleaming spokes in their huge front wheels. That wheel was as tall as he was. He couldn't imagine how anyone could boost himself way up onto the seat, then stretch down and reach the pedals and keep the whole thing balanced.

Most of the bicycles were regular safety ones like Ben's, with two wheels the same size and a chain from the back wheel to the pedals. They had big price tags: fifty, sixty dollars. One was even a hundred dollars! But it was very fancy with a wicker basket attached to the silver handlebars.

A young man approached Luc. "May I help you? Are you looking for a new bicycle?"

Luc shook his head. "No. I could never afford one of these."

"We have a few used wheels in the back. Cheaper, but still very good. Some need just a new coat of black paint. Want to look at them?"

"Yes, please." Luc followed the young man to the back of the shop.

"This one just came in. Trade-in. Pretty scratched up. I could let you have it for twenty dollars. Want to try it on for size?"

Luc straddled the bicycle, clutching the handlebars. They were scratched, and the seat was so worn you could see springs bulging through, but the bicycle was perfect! "Twenty dollars, you said? I should have that much in a few weeks. Can you keep it for me?"

"Can't promise, but folks around here aren't that keen on used bicycles these days. Everyone wants the fresh, brand-new version."

"I'll be back in a few weeks then. When I've got enough money."

The doorbell tinkled again, and a man with broad shoulders entered.

"How do, sir," the young shopkeeper said. "May I help you?"

"Aha! There you are, Luc. I thought I'd find you in here with these contraptions." It was Papa. He was frowning. "You're supposed to be out there keeping an eye on the horses. Come. We need you now. The doctor's arrived."

Luc mumbled thanks to the shopkeeper and followed Papa out. His father stopped to pat the horses' necks and tell them they wouldn't be long. The animals snorted and nodded their great heads as though they understood.

Papa turned to Luc. "The doctor's examining Joseph now. We want to be sure we understand everything he says."

The doctor's office was in the front parlour of his house beside the waiting room. It was lit by an oil lamp hanging from the ceiling. Joseph was lying on a narrow table covered with a white sheet, and Maman stood beside him, holding his hand. Although Joseph's red cheeks were streaked with tears, he was awake now and he had stopped crying. He was distracted by a small ball that rattled when he shook it.

The doctor was a tall, thin man with grey hair and round spectacles. He looked up with kind eyes as Luc and Papa entered the room.

"This is other son, Luc," Papa said. "He know all the English. More than Maman and me."

"Good. Tell your parents that it looks like your brother's leg is broken right here, just above the ankle, the tibia bone. I'd like to put a plaster cast on it to protect the leg so it'll heal straight."

Luc nodded and explained to his parents.

Maman wanted to know how long the cast would have to stay on the baby's leg, so Luc asked the doctor.

"Six weeks is the usual time," he said. "I'm sure it'll heal well. He's such a young child, and his bones are growing quickly now. But it's very important to set his leg nice and straight, or he'll never learn to walk correctly."

"We take *bébé* to hospital?" Papa asked.

"Oh, no. I can put the plaster cast on right here in the office. Excuse me. I'll get all the equipment." The doctor was back soon with a tray of instruments and materials. The old woman accompanied him. She was surprisingly gentle with Joseph, murmuring to calm him as the doctor pulled a white stocking over the baby's leg and foot. He then wrapped the stocking with layers of white gauze.

"Now comes the fun part. This is plaster powder. It needs to be mixed with water, then we'll paint it on Joseph's leg cast. In a while it'll harden, and soon he'll be almost as good as new. Here, maybe you can help mix this up for me?" the doctor asked Papa.

Luc helped Papa mix the plaster powder with some water from a jug in a large basin until the mixture was a thick, smooth paste. Then the doctor added more layers of gauze dipped into the paste until he had covered the little boy's leg from the knee down to his toes with plaster.

"Now that's what I call a good-looking cast," he said finally. "We'll let it dry for half an hour or so, then you can take him home. Now let me take a look at those scratches on your legs, Luc. They look pretty nasty. You can sit up here beside your brother."

Luc was surprised the doctor had even noticed his scraped legs.

After the doctor washed the plaster from his hands, he carefully cleaned out most of the cinders embedded in Luc's shins. "I'll put on some of this iodine. It'll sting, so hang on now."

The iodine really stung, but Luc bit his bottom lip so he wouldn't groan. Soon both his shins and knees were painted a bright orange.

"Now they shouldn't get infected," the doctor said.

Luc's parents were looking mystified, so Luc explained everything to them in French.

"It sounds as if you have a way with languages, Luc," the doctor told him "Your parents are lucky to have you help them with the English."

Lucky? Luc didn't think his parents were lucky to have him at all. He caused them nothing but trouble.

When the plaster cast was dry, the doctor said, "Now the baby's leg should heal just fine. Bring him back in six weeks and we'll cut off the cast. Meanwhile, please don't hesitate to call me if you have any concerns at all."

After thanking the doctor profusely and paying him, Papa carried Joseph out to the cart. Then they all started out on the long journey home along the deeply rutted road.

11

Luc Confronts His Fear

A few days later, when Papa came home from the stables in the evening, he announced, "A very busy day tomorrow. They need every horse and teamster they can get to go into the woods. They want to take out as many logs as they can before the winter rains set in and make the whole forest a big mudhole. We'll tow the logs down here with the horses, or haul them to the river so they can float downstream to the mill."

The next morning Papa and Rita left for the stables before it was light. Maman had risen with them to make a pot of porridge and another of tea on the campfire. Luc could hear her talking with the Poiriers, who were also early risers. He pushed himself deeper into his blankets. He didn't have to work at the office today, so he could stay in bed a while longer. It was cold and damp in the boxcar, but cozy in his bedroll.

His little brother was awake, though. He tossed and turned in his makeshift bed beside Luc and whimpered fretfully.

Luc leaned over and whispered, "Go back to sleep, Joey-boy. Go to sleep. It's still too early to get up." He tried to pat his brother's back, but the little boy wouldn't stop crying. Luc pulled himself out of his bedroll and called his mother. "Joey's awake and I don't think he's feeling very well."

Maman came back into the boxcar. "What's the matter this morning, *petit chou*?" She gathered Joseph into her arms, but he still cried. "He feels very hot. Like he has a temperature. Could you get me a cloth dipped in cool water for his head, Luc?"

But the cool cloth didn't help. As the morning wore on, Joseph became more and more fussy. His broken leg seemed to have swollen, and the cast was so tight that it was hurting him. He tugged fretfully at the plaster where the top of the cast enclosed his leg. Maman tried to placate him by rocking him and singing to him, but to no avail. He seemed to get worse and worse. Nothing she did seemed to help. He tossed and turned and cried.

"We must take him back to the doctor," Maman said finally. "I just don't know what this could be."

Madame Poirier agreed. "The sooner the doctor sees him, the better."

"But how will we get him there?" Luc asked. "Papa said they've taken every available horse into the woods today to get the logs out. There won't be any horses or carts left at the stables."

"I don't know." Maman frowned worriedly at her youngest. "Maybe we could ask the doctor to come here. I think he comes to the mill sometimes."

"I'll go to the office," Luc said. "Maybe Mr. Rogers will know how to get a message to him."

Luc grabbed his coat and cap and raced through the morning gloom to the office. When he got there, the office door was still locked. He raced around to the back door and banged on it.

It was opened by Ben's sister, Ruth. For a second Luc forgot what he was there for. He gazed into her deep blue eyes, and his heart fluttered all over the place. *Ruth Victoria* was all he could think. A wisp of her flowery fragrance enveloped him.

"Oh, hello," she said cheerfully. Her long blond hair ruffled gently in the breeze. "You're Luc, right? Ben's at school this morning. He won't be home until this afternoon. I should be at school, too, but Mother needed me this morning."

Luc cleared his throat. "Yes. Yes, I know. Your father? Is he here?"

"No. He's gone up to the woods with the lumberjacks. They have some emergency or something up there."

"Oh." Luc didn't know what to say or what to do.

"Is there something I could do to help?" She pulled on a blue sweater over her pale pink dress.

Luc shook his head to clear it. The doctor. He must get the doctor. "It's my little brother, Joey. He's sick. Very sick with a high temperature. We need to get the doctor. Right away."

"Maybe you could ride my father's horse to fetch the doctor. Chaser's in the stable down there." She pointed to the end of the garden.

"Your father's horse?" Luc stepped back, and his voice cracked. "Oh, no, I could never …"

"My father wouldn't mind. Since it's an emergency and all. Look, I'll come and help you saddle him up." She skipped lightly down the steps and along the garden path to the stable.

"But, but …" Luc said, gulping. He had no choice. He had to follow her.

When his eyes became used to the darkness in the stable, he saw a light-coloured horse nodding its head up and down. Compared to the huge Clydesdales his father worked with, this horse was as small as a pony. It had a long mane and a sprinkling of grey hairs around its muzzle. It snorted a greeting at them.

"And good morning to you, Chaser." Ruth patted the horse's head. "His saddle and saddle blanket are over there by the window." She nodded toward the equipment rack.

"Maybe I should take the buggy?" Luc suggested, his voice squeaking.

"If you ride him, you'll get to the doctor's office much faster." Ruth slipped on the horse's bridle. "Besides, Chaser is very smart and knows the way into town. He's probably made the trip a thousand times at least. Just give him a carrot when you get there."

Luc forced himself to fetch the saddle and saddle blanket from the equipment rack. His knees felt weak, but he swallowed hard and kept going, one foot in front of the other. *You can do this*, he told himself. *You can fetch the saddle and saddle blanket.* He carried them to Ruth and helped her put the blanket on the horse first, then the saddle. Finally, he cinched the saddle tightly around the horse's belly. He could do that, too.

"There. All ready." Ruth flashed him a smile.

Luc's heart lurched again. "I-It's been a long time since I've ridden a horse."

"We'll lead him outside and you can get on him there. Just a second, I'll get a carrot from the gunny sack for you to give him."

Luc shoved the carrot deep into his coat pocket. "Are you sure your father won't mind me taking him?"

"I'm sure. This is an emergency, right?"

So there was no way Luc could avoid it. He would have to ride this horse. And that was that.

He held the stable doors open while Ruth led the horse past him and outside. Luc felt the animal's huge and dangerous heat, and pulled his coat tightly around his neck. The horse stopped and waited.

Now was the moment of truth. Luc took a deep breath. A voice echoed in his head. Leo's voice. *You can do it, Luc. You can do it. Lift your foot, put it into the stirrup. Grip the saddle.*

Luc put his left foot into the stirrup, gripped the reins in one hand and the back of the saddle with the other, and swung into the saddle. Suddenly, he was so high that the top of his head grazed the overhanging branches. He hung on to the reins with all his strength, but the horse didn't move. It stood there calmly, waiting.

"He's pretty old, but he's really a lovely horse to ride," Ruth said, patting the horse's neck. "Just tug gently on the reins, and he'll know which way to go."

"Could you go and tell my mother that I've gone to fetch the doctor?" Luc's heart was crashing all over the place, but he tried to keep his voice calm. "She'll be in that boxcar, the one across the tracks from the station."

"Yes, I'll do that." Then she gave the horse a light slap on the rear, and it jerked and trotted away from the stable and up the driveway.

Branches and the side of the house flashed by Luc's face. His heart continued to beat fiercely. He bobbed in the saddle and hung on to the reins. As long as he was able to stay on the horse, he would be fine, he told himself. As long as he didn't fall off, the horse wouldn't trample him. Luc bounced up and down like a ball in the saddle. He had to get to the doctor's fast. Maybe his little brother's life depended on it.

Chaser trotted out of the yard and down to the road. Luc bowed his head and urged the horse forward, patting its neck. "Come on, boy. You can do it. We can do it," he muttered over and over, trying to make his body move with the horse's, hearing Leo's voice in his head again.

Despite the cool morning, he was sweating hard now, perspiration running down his forehead and into his eyes. He brushed it aside and saw that the road away from the townsite was muddy and filled with puddles, so he tried to ride on the verge, but the horse seemed to prefer wallowing in the mud in the middle of the road. More than once they came to a complete standstill in front of a wide puddle, and Luc had to urge the horse forward again with his knees.

"Come on, boy. We can do it. We can do it." The rhythm of the horse's movement became almost hypnotic, and eventually Luc relaxed into it.

After a while the woods closed around the road and it became a single-tracked trail. Luc didn't remember the road to Sapperton being so narrow when he made the trip a few days before in the cart with Papa. Could they have taken a wrong turn? But they hadn't made any turns at all. None that he could remember, anyway. This certainly didn't look like the same road. The farther they went along, the surer Luc was that they must have made a wrong turn somewhere.

It began to rain, first one drop falling on Luc's cheek, then another and another. Soon it was pouring hard. Luc pulled his coat tighter and the brim of his cap lower. At least the overhanging trees gave them a bit of shelter. Should he try to turn the horse around? He wasn't sure how. The horse seemed determined about its destination. It just put its head down and kept clomping along at a steady pace.

Luc didn't know what to do. Maybe he would just go along until they met someone, then he could ask directions. But they didn't meet any other travellers. Not a single one. Where was everyone today? Had they really all gone into the woods to get that last cut of the year out before the winter rains set in?

Eventually, the road widened again and the woods fell away. There was one cottage with a bit of grass around it, then another, and another. Then a whole row of houses and some other buildings.

Luc grinned. Yes! The village! This must be Sapperton. The little horse trudged onto the main road. Now what? Luc wondered. How would he get the horse to stop?

But he needn't have worried. The horse turned off the road and halted right in front of the post office. Luc was so happy that he could have hugged Chaser. Instead he slid off the horse's back and pulled the carrot out of his pocket.

"There you are, old horse."

Chaser lapped up the carrot with his long grey tongue, then Luc tied the reins to the hitching post.

"Thanks, old pal." He patted the horse's warm, furry neck.

The horse nodded and seemed to smile at Luc. Luc grinned back, then left to run along the boardwalk to the doctor's office. He burst into the office. No one was in the waiting room, but the doctor was in his examining room, sitting at his desk and reading a thick book.

"Doctor!" Luc cried out, his voice hoarse. "It's my little brother! He's very sick. A high temperature."

"Hold on there, son," Dr. Scott said. "Sit down a minute. I'll get you a drink of water. Now what's the problem?"

Soon after, Dr. Scott fetched his horse and buggy and was on his way to the mill townsite. Luc untied

Chaser. "Home," he said to the horse. "Home we go."

The horse nodded as though it understood. Luc swung into the saddle, and they followed the doctor's buggy down the main road and out of the village.

Amazing! Now Luc wasn't scared of the horse at all. In fact, he felt quite comfortable, easing into the steady rhythm of the animal's stride as they clomped along the narrow road through the bush.

When they approached the mill townsite, the doctor stopped his horse and waited until Luc drew up beside him. "You'll have to direct me to your house from here."

"We're living in the boxcar across the tracks from the train station."

"A boxcar? I've never heard of anyone living in a boxcar."

"It's really not too bad. Except when the wind blows the rain in. Then sometimes our stuff gets pretty wet."

The doctor shook his head as he turned his horse down the road leading to the station. Luc was right behind him. When they got to the station, they tied the horses to a tree beside the tracks. Luc led the doctor to the boxcar where Maman was sitting on the trunk, holding Joseph wrapped in her shawl. She was rocking him and crooning a lullaby. Clara was sitting beside her, cradling her dolly and singing, too.

"Well, now, what do we have here? Two sick babies?" The doctor smiled down at Clara, and she smiled back at him, her usual shyness gone. Luc thought that he would have to remember that trick when he was a doctor himself.

After examining Clara's doll, especially her ears, Dr. Scott examined Joseph. He said that it looked as if the broken leg was causing an inflammation, and he gave Maman some medicine for the little boy.

"It'll take a few hours to work, but by this evening he should be feeling much better. We get this sometimes with broken limbs."

Maman turned to Luc, and he explained what the doctor had said. She nodded. "But my *bébé*, he will be fine?"

The doctor nodded. "Yes, he should be just fine, Madame Godin. It's a good thing your son got me so quickly, though. It's best to treat these fevers as soon as we can."

Maman smiled at Luc and patted his arm. "He is my big boy," she said proudly.

Luc ducked his head. She didn't know how scared he had been.

The doctor was looking around the boxcar. By now it was tidy and swept out daily, and several blankets had been hung about on ropes, making the whole area cozier. But the doctor shook his head. "This isn't a good place for families with young ones to be living. It's much too damp, especially in winter. It'll soon get colder and wetter until it'll be quite impossible without heat. It's a wonder your children aren't sick all the time. I'll see if there's something I can do about it. I'll talk to Mr. Rogers and some people in town, as well."

This time Maman seemed to understand most of what the doctor was saying.

"Not only my family," she told him. "Three other family, they live in boxcar, too. The Poiriers, the Boileaus, and the Leblancs."

After promising he would see what he could do for the four families, the doctor left.

12

The Doctor's Magic

It was as though Dr. Scott had waved a magic wand. A week or so later a building crew from Sapperton arrived at the townsite, and with all the lumber they needed close by at the mill, they started building four small houses in a row, south of the tracks and down the street leading to the river. Everyone worked long hours, lighting the dark nights with smoky torches. Even the bachelors, the rough lumberjacks, pitched in after they put in a full day's work in the woods or at the mill. Papa's friend, Le Gros, got them all to come and help by promising them a big party when the houses were completed.

Luc and his friends, Ben and Harry, and some other boys their age, fetched and carried and also held up the smoky torches so the carpenters could work far into the night. Ben and Harry even had a few days off school to help out, so they were pretty happy.

It took several weeks, but finally, a few days before Christmas, the houses were ready for occupation. They were all the same. A broad front door led to a big room that would be used as a parlour and kitchen. In the centre of the left wall was a big cooking stove that heated the whole house with plenty of firewood from off-cuts from the mill. At the back of the house were two small bedrooms and a closet that held a portable toilet.

They would have to wait until the spring to paint the houses because paint would never dry in the damp coastal air at that time of the year. Right now, though, the little houses were snug and cozy and dry. And with the fog and rain that continued day after day, that was what mattered. The carpenters had even provided some basic furniture.

Finally, it was moving day! Le Gros and Papa, lugging the Godins' big family trunk, led a parade of the four families from the boxcar, across the tracks, and past the shops to their new houses.

Madame Leblanc and her daughters were dressed in fancy new clothes for the event — all frilly dresses and hats and shiny high-button shoes. Of course, the only things they carried were their small handbags and tiny wicker baskets.

Luc had a heavy carpet bag in each hand and another slung over his shoulder. He followed Rita across the tracks. She was balancing an enormous bundle of blankets on her head.

As they approached the narrow plank walkway that led across the muddy swamp to the new houses, the Leblanc girls pushed ahead of Luc. Then Louisa nudged Rita out of the way with her elbow. Rita stumbled, but she managed to stay upright and hold on to her load as Isabella ploughed past her, as well.

"I'm going to see our new house first!" Isabella squealed, racing her sister to the plank walkway.

"Oh, no, you're not!" Louisa shouted. "I am!" She glanced over her shoulder at her sister and started to scamper along the narrow planks.

Whether Isabella pushed Louisa, or Louisa pushed Isabella, Luc wasn't sure. The next thing he knew, they were both tumbling off the narrow walkway into the muddy swamp. *Plop! Plop!*

"*Eeek!*" one squealed.

"Get me out!" cried the other. "Oh, it's so mucky! So dirty! Help!"

The girls wailed and struggled in the mud, waving their arms and knees.

"Rita!" one demanded. "You get us out of here right this instant!"

"So sorry," Rita said. "My hands are full. And I'm sure Maman wouldn't like our bedding to get all wet and muddy for our brand-new house." She swished past the two girls.

Luc could tell she was trying hard not to grin. He shrugged at the girls, too, and followed his sister, being extra careful to keep to the narrow plank walkway.

The girls continued screaming as they wallowed in the swamp up to their thighs. Their fancy skirts and petticoats became soaked with mud and strewn with weeds. The harder they struggled, the muddier they got.

"You two come back here!" they yelled. "Come and help us at once!"

Luc shook his head and tried his hardest to keep from laughing. He hurried away, past the first three new houses. Finally, he got to the fourth one. As he turned off onto another even narrower walkway, he couldn't contain himself any longer. Hoots of laughter burst out of him. Then Rita started laughing, too, and he laughed even harder until he almost lost his balance and fell into the mud, as well.

When they finally made it to their front door, Luc saw that Rita had tears in her eyes, she had been laughing so hard.

"Serves those two darn right," she said.

Luc nodded. "Yes siree." He took a deep breath and pushed the door open with his shoulder.

"Ah, there you two are!" Maman cried. "Isn't this so beautiful! *La maison! Comme c'est belle!*" She was holding little Joseph in her arms and twirling him about until the skirt of her long blue dress ballooned around her. "It's all so beautiful! Beautiful! I just can't believe it! I love it! I love it! After all this time, finally, we have our own little house!" Her eyes were shining, and she blinked back tears as she put the little boy down on the wooden plank floor in the middle of the parlour.

Grunting, Papa and Le Gros pushed the big trunk beside the front window.

"*Merci, mon ami*," Papa said. "You tell the boys that we'll have that big party soon. Maybe right after Christmas."

"The sooner, the better." The big man shook his hand and left.

Maman opened the trunk and rummaged around. She pulled out a rectangular parcel wrapped in one of her scarves, the soft blue one. The parcel was a large photograph in an ornate wooden frame. "I think we should hang this in a special place. Here, right beside the front window."

Papa hammered a nail into the wall beside the front window with the blunt end of his axe.

Maman kissed the photograph and hung it on the nail. "Now we're all here together, the whole family, in our own little house."

Papa hugged her shoulders and gazed at the photograph with her. "Yes," he said softly, kissing the top of her head. "We're all together again."

Luc piled his carpet bags beside the old trunk and stared up at the photograph, too. It had been taken just before Christmas a year ago. In it Papa, Rita, and Clara stood beside Maman, who was seated with baby Joseph in her arms. And behind her, with his hand on Luc's shoulder, stood Leo. Luc was stunned at how alike they looked. Both he and his brother were grinning broadly with identical grins at the photographer as though they were sharing a joke. Luc couldn't remember what the joke was, but looking at the photograph made a smile twitch at his lips. He did remember how Leo always made him laugh, made everyone laugh. How he would have howled at the two fancy Leblanc sisters struggling in the mucky swamp!

Who would have ever imagined that a year could have made such a difference to their family?

Luc took a deep breath and looked around the house. It was fresh and clean, and after the confined space of the boxcar, it seemed enormous. Best of all, the house would be for just his family. Not a Leblanc girl in sight. He thought Leo would have appreciated that, as well.

Clara propped her dolly up on the trunk and joined Rita galloping around the house and squealing with delight. Joseph joined them, too, crawling after them, grinning and drooling. Now that his leg was out of the cast, Dr. Scott said it was completely healed, but Joseph was still cautious about using it for walking, preferring to crawl instead.

"Our parlour," Maman was saying. "And our kitchen. Look, they've made a good solid table for us, and benches all around. And the cook stove! Have you ever in your life, seen such a magnificent stove?" The stove was shiny black with a smokestack that went into the ceiling. "Look, there's even a warming oven where I can put the bread to rise. Oh, the dinners I will make here!"

"Look! Beds!" Rita whooped, racing into one of the back rooms. "They even have real beds for us! No more sleeping on the ground. That room can be for you and Papa, Maman, and this one will be for us!"

Clara squealed as she followed Rita to one of the beds. They both climbed up and stretched out on it. "Exactly the right size," Rita declared.

"Right size," Clara echoed.

It was just a bare mattress, but compared to what they'd had to sleep on in the boxcar for the past few months, it was the height of luxury.

"We can put pictures on the walls and have some pillows all around," Rita told Clara. "Make our room all fancy, fancy."

"Fancy, fancy!" Clara echoed.

"Humph," Luc said. "Maybe I could have a bed in the parlour or something?" He hated the idea of having to share a room with his sisters.

"I know," Maman said. "What about the attic for you? When I was a girl growing up in Quebec, that's where my brothers always liked to sleep."

"There's an attic here?"

Maman pointed to a big square trap door in the ceiling beside the stovepipe.

"How would I get up there?"

"I think the builders left a ladder in the back," Papa said.

Sure enough, a tall ladder was leaning against the back of their house beside a load of firewood.

Papa and Luc carried the ladder inside and leaned it against the wall. Luc scrambled up and pushed on the trap door. It gave way, and he boosted himself through the hole and looked around.

It was a big space with a low ceiling that followed the slant of the roof. Above the cook stove it would be warm and cozy. And private. His own world. There was even a small air vent to let in some light.

"How is it, Luc?" Maman asked from below.

"It'll be just great." He climbed back down the ladder to get his bag and bedroll.

"Good. Now bring my dishes and pots and pans over here," Maman directed. "We'll put them on these shelves." She looked around, smiling. "Isn't this all so wonderful! And just in time for Christmas. If we had some green boughs and maybe even a bit of holly, we could put them around the windows and I could put some candles here and there. Oh, my! Everything will look so festive."

"I could get some greenery from the woods tomorrow, Maman," Luc said. "It's Sunday, so I don't have to work at the office."

"And I could help you, Luc," Rita said.

"That would be wonderful," Maman said. "Let's try out our new stove. How about some crepes for supper to celebrate?"

"Crepes! Yum!" Luc said. They hadn't had crepes for ages, not since they'd left their old home in Quebec months before. And the big, thin pancakes rolled up with maple sugar or strawberry *confiture* were everyone's favourite supper.

"Come and give me a hand, Luc," Papa said. "I'll chop a load of firewood and we'll get a good hot fire going in Maman's glorious new cook stove. Can't wait to taste those crepes."

13

Searching for the Perfect Tree

The next afternoon after Sunday Mass, which was held in a room above the general store, Luc was restless. Maman and Papa stayed on to visit with some of their old friends who had settled in the village of Port Moody, over the hill, and had come to Fraser Mills for the Sunday service. It was hot and stuffy above the store. The Mass, celebrated by the visiting priest, had been long and boring, particularly the sermon about hell-fire and brimstone and how everyone must always be on the lookout for the presence of *le diable*, who lurked among them, tempting them into evil ways.

Outside it was actually not raining for a change, and Luc wanted to get out there. "Hey, Rita! You want to go up to the woods now and collect some greenery to decorate the house?"

"Good idea. I'll just tell Maman."

Maman waved goodbye, and Luc and Rita left.

They started up through the village toward the woods, but Luc stopped. He had an idea. "Wait here. I want to get something from home." He raced back along the boardwalk and got Papa's axe from beside the wood pile behind the house.

Rita jogged after him. "Won't Papa be awfully mad if you take his axe? You know how he doesn't like anyone touching it."

"I'd ask him, but he's so busy talking to his friends. Besides, I have a plan and I want it to be a surprise."

"What's the plan?"

"I was thinking that we could find a Christmas tree, chop it down, bring it back, and set it up in the parlour. Wouldn't that be great?"

"A Christmas tree! Yes!" she shouted. "I'm sure we can find the perfect one in the woods. There are so many trees there."

But they tramped on for quite a while along the narrow trail that led deep into the forest north of the village without finding what they wanted. The forest was made up of mostly tall dark evergreen trees, but there were also alders and maples with very few leaves left on their spindly branches.

"We'll never find a good tree," Rita grumbled, kicking at soggy maple leaves that littered the path. "They're all either way too big or way too small and scrawny. Besides, I'm hungry. It must be almost suppertime now. Let's just cut some green branches to hang around the windows in the parlour, like Maman said."

"You didn't have to come, you know. You could have stayed home. And it can't be suppertime yet. The mill whistle hasn't blown. Besides, you agreed that we should get a good tree for Christmas to surprise everyone." Luc swung Papa's axe at a spindly alder tree blocking the trail. Papa's axe was so sharp that it cut through the wood as if it were soap, toppling the tree.

Rita stopped dead. "There it is!" She pointed through the clearing Luc had made. "That's got to be the perfect tree!"

In the dying light of the afternoon, the pale green fir tree stood out from the surrounding foliage on a rise in the forest. It had a regular shape and plenty of thick branches.

"You're right. Looks like the best one yet."

They scrambled to the tree through ferns, underbrush, and dwarf alders. Prickly branches clawed at Luc's face and sleeves. When they got closer, he saw that the tree was several feet taller than he was, and its thick branches grew right to the ground.

He chopped away the bush and vines around the tree so they could get a better look at it. "It's a good size, but it'll be hard to get to the trunk to chop it down. There are so many low branches."

"Maybe you'll have to chop off some of them," Rita suggested. "It'll still be plenty tall enough."

The narrow, springy branches near the ground were easy to chop off. One or two swings of Papa's sharp axe was all it took. It was a good thing Papa's axe was so sharp. The thick trunk, though, was a different matter.

"Hurry up, Luc," Rita urged. "It'll be dark soon."

"I'm going as fast as I can." Luc was breathing heavily from exertion now. When he hit the trunk straight across, the axe blade just bounced back. He had to hit the tree at an angle to cut into the wood. Every time he swung the axe the tree shivered and showered them with damp needles that went down Luc's back. Soon he was sweating, and his hands stung with blisters.

"One last swing and that should do it." He brushed sweat from his forehead and swung the axe with all his strength. The blade bit into the wood, and the little tree finally toppled over onto its side.

"Good, that's it," Rita said. "Sure smells lovely. So sweet and clean. It'll be perfect for the parlour. Maman and the little kids will love it."

"I'll take the bottom of the trunk and you hold it at the top." Luc put his shoulder under the tree trunk and lifted. It was a lot heavier than he had expected. "All right? You got it? Let's get it back onto the trail."

They dragged the tree through the bushes, Luc leading. He ducked to avoid the sharp prickles of the underbrush. "Hold it a minute." He stopped. "I just remembered something. I left Papa's axe behind."

"Oh, no! He'll be really mad if we lose it."

"Wait here. I'll get it." Luc pushed back through the prickly bush. The white of the freshly cut trunk flashed in the gloom. Right beside it rested Papa's axe. He heaved a sigh of relief. Rita was right. Papa would be so angry if he lost his axe. As he bent to retrieve it, the bush beside him moved.

He caught his breath and stared. A wild animal, like a bear or cougar, flashed through his head. This was, after all, the Wild West. And there were those bear droppings he and Papa had seen beside the train tracks. He grabbed the axe, gulped hard, and held it ready to fight for his life.

He waited, frozen. Nothing happened. Whatever it was it must have slunk away into the shadows. Maybe now it was heading for Rita!

Luc rushed back to his sister. She was sitting on a mossy mound beside their tree, alone. Relief washed over him again. But they had to get out of these woods before any wild animals found them. He grabbed the base of their tree and plunged into the underbrush, dragging it behind him.

"Luc, I don't think that's the way to the trail," Rita said, lifting the top of the tree and following him. "Wasn't it over that way?"

"I'm sure it's straight ahead."

"If it was, we should be there already," she grumbled.

"Let's go on just a bit farther." He continued to hurry through the underbrush, tripping over mossy logs and bunches of ferns. They trudged on for a while, but they still didn't come to the trail.

"It's getting darker, Luc. Soon we won't be able to see where we're going."

"Quit your complaining. Can't you hold your end up any higher?"

They stumbled along but didn't make much headway. With each step the bush seemed to get thicker and harder to push through.

"Let's stop and rest for a minute," Rita puffed behind him.

Luc stopped reluctantly. He opened his eyes as wide as he could and wished he could see better in the gathering gloom. Everywhere he looked was the same — thick, tangled bush, tall trees with broad bases, moss-covered ground, patches of fern. "I was sure this was the right way." He scratched the back of his neck.

"We're not lost, are we?" Rita asked, a tremble in her voice.

"No, no." Luc shook his head. "I don't think so, anyway."

Rita pulled herself up onto a broad stump and took a good look around. "I still can't see where the trail is," she said, straining to see through the woods.

They had stopped beside an old cedar tree with broad branches that grew right to the ground.

"I could climb up this tree. Then maybe I could get a good look around," Luc said, pulling his cap lower on his forehead. He pushed through the big tree's lower branches to its broad trunk. The branches stuck out at regular intervals.

"Hey, Rita," he called through the thick foliage. "This tree's easy to climb, easy as a ladder." He pulled himself up onto another branch. As he made his way upward from branch to branch, he kept his head lowered to avoid the bits of bark and needles falling into his face.

"I'm coming up, too," Rita said.

"No. You better wait down there. You might fall."

"What if a cougar comes along? Or a wolf or a bear or something? No, I'm coming up, too."

He didn't argue. It was probably safer if they kept together. "Just be careful not to fall."

They both climbed up and up. At first the tree felt as solid as a church building, but as they climbed higher and neared the top, the trunk became so narrow that it swayed back and forth in the darkness. With each step it rocked more and more, making Luc dizzy.

"We're high enough now, don't you think?" Luc grabbed the narrow trunk with both hands and peered out through the branches. The branches were so thin way up here that he could see out over the forest. Up so high it felt as if they were almost touching the clouds. Except for the wind it was totally silent. Then he heard something!

"Did you hear that?" he hissed. The flesh on the back of his neck prickled and his heart lurched and pounded.

"Wolves!" Rita breathed. "Sounds like a pack of howling wolves."

"Wolves. Or coyotes maybe. They howl, too, I think."

"Or maybe it's *le diable* himself coming to get us for taking Papa's axe."

The eerie calls floated on the darkness, drifting up to them.

"It sounds closer now," Luc whispered, shivering. "They must be coming this way. Maybe they smelled or heard us. Maybe they were following us all the time."

"What should we do? Should we stay up here in the tree? We're safe up here, right? Wolves can't climb trees, can they?"

"But devils probably can." Luc was so scared that he couldn't think. Sweat trickled down his back and from his forehead into his eyes. He brushed it away with the back of his hand.

"I see it!" Rita squealed. "I see the river. That must be it. Right? See that glint of grey, way over there?"

"Where?" Luc blinked hard and stared into the darkness.

"Over there. No, you're looking the wrong way. That way!" She pointed at a glint of grey through the forest canopy.

"You're right. That must be the Fraser River." Rita always did have the sharpest eyes. "And the mill and our new house will be right there, too. So that's the direction we have to go."

"Can you remember?"

"I think so. *Shh!* Listen." Now all he could hear was the night wind sighing through the high branches. No more howling.

"I can't hear them anymore, can you?" Rita asked.

He held his breath and listened really hard. "No. But that doesn't mean they've gone. They could be right there at the bottom of the tree, waiting for us to come down. Waiting to pounce on us."

"What do you want to do?"

"I don't know. We can't stay up here all night."

"I'm going to chance it," Rita said. "I'm going down."

Luc couldn't let her go off by herself. What if a big pack of wolves really was waiting for them at the bottom of the tree? They would tear her to bits. Or it could be something even more terrible. "Wait. You can't go down there by yourself."

But she didn't stop or even look up at him. So he had to follow her. He took a deep breath and started descending, scrambling from limb to limb down to the lowest branches.

"Wait a second," Luc hissed.

"What for?"

"The wolves. They might be waiting for us at the bottom of the tree."

Rita pushed the branches aside and peered down at the ground. "Can't see any wolves down there. Or anything else. I'm going." And before he could stop her, she swung on the low branch and jumped the rest of the way to the ground. "It's fine, Luc. No wolves down here. Or devils, either."

He swung down and joined her. He squinted into the gloom. If there were any animals around, it was too dark to see them now, though he could make out the mound of their Christmas tree.

"All set?" He grabbed the base. "Let's get going. This way, right?" He shouldered the trunk and pushed through the surrounding bushes as fast as he could, dragging the tree behind him.

Rita scrambled after him. "Wait up, Luc. I can't even see where I'm going."

But he didn't stop until he stumbled upon a clearing. "It's the trail!" Luc grinned back at her. "We found the trail!"

"Finally!"

The going was so much easier that Luc relaxed and

strode along the trail with long steps. The tree didn't even feel all that heavy now. That was when he remembered something.

"Oh, no!" he groaned, stopping in his tracks. "I forgot Papa's axe again. This time beside the big cedar. Papa will be so mad if we lose it. We better go back for it."

"We can't, Luc. It's getting so dark that we can barely see where we're going. And those wolves might be there now. I think we should just get home as fast as we can. Can't you come back here tomorrow morning and look for it? I'll tie my hair ribbon right here and you'll know where to turn off the trail."

"You're right, I guess. I sure wouldn't like to meet those wolves face-to-face in the dark."

Rita pulled the white hair ribbon from her braid and tied it to a branch of a spindly alder beside the trail. "When you come back tomorrow morning, you'll see the ribbon and know exactly where to go."

"Right." But now Luc's feet felt so heavy that he could barely lift them. Papa would be really angry. That was his favourite axe. And as he had told Luc, to a woodsman, his axe was his most important tool.

14

Savage Attack

"Slow down, Luc. I can't keep up," Rita panted from behind him. Her voice was muffled by the fir tree they were both carrying.

"But it's so late. They'll be so worried. I should have gone back for Papa's axe."

"You can get it in the morning. You know right where you left it."

They were out of the forest now and jogging through the village. Luc stopped at the railway tracks and checked left and right. There were no trains in sight, so he crossed over and headed for the narrow boardwalk that led to their new house. It was a temporary walkway that the men had laid over the muddy swamp surrounding the new houses. Just the width of a board, it was so narrow that staying on it carrying the broad tree felt like walking a tightrope.

"Be careful not to step off the boards," he told his sister. "There's deep mud down there after all this rain."

"They're going to be so surprised when they see our tree. We must be almost there."

"Yes! There's the Boileaus' house, and the Leblancs'. Just one more to go. And here we are." Luc turned onto another boardwalk that Papa and he had made a couple of days before. Warm yellow light poured out of the two front windows of their new house, one on either side of the door. Maman had lit the candles on the window ledges. Maybe Papa wouldn't be home yet and Luc would have time to think up a good reason why he had left his father's axe up in the bush.

Luc climbed the three steps up to the front door and pushed it open. He pulled in the fir tree, forcing it through the doorway into the parlour. Rita was right behind him.

"Surprise!" they both shouted.

"Oh, my!" Maman's hands flew to her cheeks. "What do you have there?"

Luc raised the tree and propped it up in the corner by the window.

"A Christmas tree," Rita said. "Don't you just love it!"

Clara's dark eyes were as big as plums. "Oh!" she breathed. "A tree for Christmas!"

Rita grabbed her hands, and they spun around the parlour squealing with delight.

"It's beautiful!" Maman said. "So fresh and green, and it smells like the whole forest. I'll get a bucket you can put it in. With some rocks to help it stay upright, that will be lovely. But I was getting worried about you two. It's so late. I was wondering what was taking you so long, but now I see what it was. Papa went to the stables to check on the horses, but he'll be home soon for supper."

So Papa wasn't home yet. Luc breathed a sigh of relief.

But just then there were footsteps on the stairs and the front door was pushed open again.

"Papa!" Clara shrieked, running to him. Her cheeks were red with excitement. "Look! Look, Papa! We have a tree for Christmas!"

"Eh, but that's a beauty!" He picked Clara up and twirled her around. "Now where did that one come from?"

"Luc and Rita got it up in the woods," Maman said. "I was going to get a bucket to put the trunk in."

"And a thick trunk that is." Papa examined the bottom. "It must have taken some chopping to get through that one."

Luc swallowed hard. He might as well get it over with right now. "Papa, there's something I have to tell you. I borrowed your axe this afternoon."

Papa put Clara down and stared at Luc, his dark eyebrows furling. "But I told you that you must never take my axe without my permission."

"Sorry, Papa. You weren't here, and Rita and I, we wanted to surprise everyone with the Christmas tree, you see."

Papa shook his head. "That's no excuse. That axe isn't a plaything to be used by children. It's a woodsman's tool. I want you to promise that you'll never take it again without my permission."

"I promise, Papa. Um, there's something else." How was he ever going to tell him now that the axe was lost?

Rita nudged him. "Now," she mouthed.

Luc's mouth was so dry that he could barely get it open. "The thing is," he mumbled. "The thing is, we left it up in the woods," he finished as fast as he could.

"What!" Papa exploded. "You left my axe in the woods! I don't believe it! Not only have you disobeyed me by taking the axe, but you've lost it, as well?"

"But … but it's not lost. Not really. I know exactly where it is, Papa. We do, right, Rita?"

Rita nodded. "We tied my hair ribbon on the trail near where we left it."

"I can go back and get it first thing in the morning," Luc said.

"If you know where it is, why didn't you bring it back with you?"

"It was getting so dark that we could barely see the trail, and ... and ..." Papa was right. He should have gone back to get it. Wild animals or not.

Papa breathed heavily and looked at Luc sternly. "Well, just see that you get it first thing in the morning before anyone else finds it. And you must never, ever, take it again without my permission."

The next morning Luc woke to the sound of heavy raindrops hammering on the roof above his head in the attic. Shivering, he slipped out of his bedroll and lifted the curtain over the narrow air vent. The sky wasn't pitch-black so that meant it would be light soon. He pulled on his pants and sweater and hurried down the ladder to the kitchen. No one else in the family was up yet. He grabbed his coat and cap from the hook by the door, tied on his boots, and let himself out as quietly as a shadow.

The rain wasn't that cold on his face, but he still lowered his head and jogged up the boardwalk, across the tracks, and through the village. Soon he was trotting along the trail they had taken the evening before. He kept his eyes open wide for a glimpse of Rita's white hair ribbon. When the trail came to a Y, he turned right, then jogged along some more. Although he was entering the deeper forest, it was getting lighter. The sun must be rising somewhere behind the thick bank of clouds. It was raining steadily, but the overhanging branches protected him.

Finally, he saw the ribbon fluttering in the distance. It was sodden with the overnight rain, but he untied it, anyway, and put it in his pocket. Rita would be glad to get it back. He left the trail and soon found the huge cedar tree they had climbed the night before. And, yes! There was Papa's axe exactly where he had left it on the ground beside the tree. So close. Why hadn't he just gone back for it the night before? Things always appeared different in the morning light.

As he was pushing his way through the underbrush back to the trail, he heard someone calling, "Here, Scottie. Come here. Come back here right this minute!" A girl's voice. It sounded like Ruth Rogers. Luc's heart skipped a beat.

"Scottie! Oh, no! Help! Help!" she screamed. "Someone help!"

Luc leaped over a stump and raced down the trail toward her voice. There she was on the trail in front of him. Screaming!

"Scotty! Oh, no! They've got my Scottie! They grabbed my Scottie! You give me back my dog right this instant!" she shrieked as she disappeared from the trail.

Luc rushed to the spot he'd last seen her. She was gone! He heard a scurrying in the bush to his right and plunged in after her.

Ruth swung around, her face white with fear. "Oh, Luc! It's you!"

"What is it? What happened?"

"My dog! My Scottie! They've got my Scottie!"

"Who? Who has him?"

"Don't know. Big dogs? I couldn't really see."

"Big dogs?"

"They came from the bushes."

"Bushes?"

"They pounced on my Scottie. Just grabbed him. Dragged him away."

There was a commotion in the underbrush to their left. Ferocious yelps and growls were followed by frantic, high-pitched squeals.

"Get him!" Ruth shouted. "We have to get him!"

Luc leaped over a fallen log and dived into the bush, coming face-to-face with two pairs of wild green eyes, a flash of dark fur, and long bushy tails. Wolves? Coyotes maybe? One of the animals had the little black dog by the scruff of the neck.

"Drop that dog!" Luc yelled fiercely. Wielding Papa's axe above his head, he attacked both wild animals with all his strength. At first the animals snarled menacingly at him, baring their long white teeth. But Luc roared, "Get away, you two! Get away!" He kicked at them and struck out with Papa's axe, first at one, then the other. After a ferocious struggle, the animal finally dropped the little dog. Then, with more low growls, both animals slunk away into the bushes.

Scottie had fallen to the ground and lay still.

Ruth pushed her way through the bushes. "Oh, my poor dear little Scottie!" She rushed to the dog's side and gathered him up in her arms. He was bleeding from a gash on his neck, but his eyes were open and he was panting.

"He's alive! He's alive!" she cried, tears streaming down her cheeks. "My Scottie's still alive!"

Luc nodded, staring into the bush, half expecting the wild animals to return. But the bushes were still. "We better get him home before they come back." He helped Ruth up and shouldered Papa's axe. Now that the struggle was over, his legs felt like water and threatened to buckle under him.

"You saved him, Luc." Ruth gazed at him with shining eyes through her tears. "You saved my dear little Scottie.

I don't know how to thank you."

Luc shrugged and stroked his trembling knees. "Good thing I had my father's axe to scare them off. Come on, let's get this poor thing home."

The girl looked at Luc with such glowing eyes that he straightened up and grew a couple of inches right there.

15

Christmas Eve

That night Luc helped Rita and Clara decorate the Christmas tree in the corner of the parlour beside the window. As Maman had said, it made the whole house smell as fresh and clean as the forest. They had trimmed off more of the tree's lower branches, which they pinned to the top of the windows and around the family photograph.

Maman was at the kitchen table rolling out pastry for the many tarts she was baking for the big celebration for their new house. They had decided to have it the day after Christmas. It was going to be for all the lumberjacks who had helped build the houses. Dr. Scott had been invited to be the guest of honour. Lum King, too, was invited for his friendship and for his help with Joseph when the little boy's leg had been broken.

Papa was sitting on a bench beside the table, playing with Joseph, trying to get him to walk. "Come on, *mon petit*," he coaxed. "You can do it."

Rita and Clara were chatting excitedly about what Papa Noël was going to bring. Maybe a treat or two for them would appear under the tree.

Luc looked around the cozy house. Something was missing. It was true that it was filled with excitement and wonderful smells. There wasn't much furniture yet. But it wasn't the lack of furniture that was the missing thing. Luc knew what it was. With a sharp pang he thought of Leo. It was as if there were a deep hole where Leo should have been. The other thing Luc missed was music. Papa's violin music. Their home in Quebec had always been filled to the brim with Leo's boisterous laughter, and with Papa's music. Music was Papa's other voice. Luc sighed. He missed hearing that voice.

The last time Papa had played his violin had been way back in September on the train when they were arriving at this townsite by the river. Since that day, the violin had lain in pieces in the old trunk. And Luc knew whose fault that was. Would Papa ever get a new one? he wondered.

"Time for bed," Maman said, putting the last batch of tarts into the oven. "Tomorrow is an important day for everyone."

Although the next day was Christmas Eve, it was work as usual for everyone at the mill, including Luc at the office.

"I'll be going to Sapperton to do some last-minute business this afternoon," Dan Rogers announced. "So we'll be closing the office at noon."

"Could I go with you?" Luc asked the manager. With the five-dollar Christmas bonus his boss had given him for saving Ruth's Scottie, Luc now had enough money to buy the bicycle he had seen weeks ago at the shop in Sapperton. Maybe he'd even have a bit of extra money left over to buy some Christmas treats for his family. The bicycle wasn't brand-new, but it was shiny and black. And when he had it, he would ride like the wind.

"Of course, Luc. I'd be glad for the company. I want to leave in —" Mr. Rogers checked his pocket watch "— half an hour."

"That'll give me time to go home and get the rest of my money."

Luc ran all the way to their new house on the other side of the tracks. It felt strange to be thinking about celebrating Christmas with not a speck of snow in sight. By now in Quebec there would be at least six inches of the white stuff covering everything with a smooth, clean white blanket, and everyone would be cleaning off their skates to go skating on the frozen Gatineau River. Here on the West Coast, though, it had rained so hard and steadily that the ground by this river had turned into a muddy swamp.

Luc burst into their little house. Delicious smells of baking met him at the door.

"Luc, you're home early." Maman was at the kitchen table, kneading a batch of bread.

"Mr. Rogers is closing the office and going to Sapperton this afternoon, so I can get a ride with him." Luc scrambled up the ladder to his room in the attic. He reached under his bed for the tobacco tin and dumped out its contents. He counted it quickly. Twenty-four dollars altogether. Plenty for the bicycle, plus a little extra for Christmas treats for the rest of the family. He rolled the bills, shoved them into his coat pocket, and hurried back down the ladder. When he got to the bottom, he gave his mother a quick kiss on the cheek, then flew out the door.

Mr. Rogers's horse, Chaser, was waiting in the driveway beside the manager's house, already hitched to the buggy. The horse impatiently pawed at the ground.

Luc patted Chaser's neck, then stroked the horse's nose where its fur was soft and velvety smooth. "Hello, old fellow." He remembered how the horse had taken him all the way to the next village to fetch the doctor. Not only that, but Chaser had taught Luc that horses weren't such scary animals, after all. He breathed in the warm animal smell and found it quite comforting.

Mr. Rogers appeared, and they were off, with Luc sitting up in the buggy beside his boss.

"So what are you going to be shopping for?" Mr. Rogers asked Luc as the horse clomped along Pitt River Road and out of the townsite.

Luc patted his pocket. "I've finally got enough money to buy myself a bicycle, and there's one at the bicycle shop that's a real beauty. It just needs a little oil and maybe a bit of paint, then it'll be almost as good as new."

"A bicycle! That'll be fun for you. Then you can go riding with Benjamin and his friends."

When they got to Sapperton, Mr. Rogers directed his horse to stop in front of the post office as usual. "It'll take me about an hour to finish all my business, then I'll be going back home. So if you want a lift, you can meet me here then."

"Thanks for the lift, sir. But I won't be needing a ride back home. Not with my new bicycle, I won't."

Luc rushed away along the broad boardwalk. He turned to go into the bicycle store when something in the window of the shop next door, Martin's, caught his eye. He stopped abruptly and stared. It was dusty and scratched, and one of the strings was broken, but it was a violin! A small card leaned against the instrument: $20.00.

He patted the bulk of rolled bills in his coat pocket, hesitating only for a second, then turned on his heel and hurried into the shop before he changed his mind.

An hour later, when Mr. Rogers returned to his horse and buggy, Luc was waiting for him. It had started to rain, so he had his coat collar turned up and his cap pulled over his forehead.

"Changed your mind about the bicycle, I see," Mr. Rogers said.

Luc nodded and followed him up to the buggy. "Got something else," he muttered. "Something better."

16

Luc's Surprise

Luc's heart was pounding. *Calm down*, he told himself as he trudged down the hill, through the townsite, and across the tracks. *You're not robbing a bank. But what if Papa doesn't like it? What if it's just a piece of old junk?* He held the violin close under his coat so the damp winter air wouldn't get to it. A thick grey fog swirled up from the river and mingled with smoke pouring out of the smokestacks at the mill.

When Luc pushed open the door to their little house, he was flooded with wonderful smells for the Christmas Eve feast when they would celebrate *le réveillon* after Midnight Mass. A plump chicken with onions and carrots and potatoes and sage was roasting in the oven of the big wood stove. And a big pan of fresh buns, crusty and golden brown, cooled on the warming oven above the stove beside a spicy gingerbread speckled with fat, juicy raisins.

Rita was helping Clara hang their last paper chain on the fir tree. The tree took up every bit of space in the corner, holding out its branches as if in prayer. They had tied on ten small rosy red apples from Lum King, and the apples twirled on their threads, catching the light from the oil lamps.

"Ah, there you are, Luc." Maman smiled at him from the table where she was peeling more of Lum King's apples for a pie. "I was starting to worry. It's already so dark with all the fog. Papa has some very good news for you."

Luc hoped that Papa wouldn't be home from work yet, but there he was, helping the girls finish decorating the tree.

"Can you help me put my star up on the tree?" Clara asked Papa. "I want it to go on the very top." She held out a lopsided paper star she had coloured using up her whole yellow crayon. It was as thick and shiny as butter.

Papa stooped to lift her. "Stand on my shoulders."

Clara squealed as Papa swung her up to his shoulders. He held on to her legs as she leaned over and tied the star to the very top branch, the one that grazed the ceiling.

"Oh, that's the most beautiful Christmas tree I've ever seen," Maman said after Papa put Clara down. "It's perfect! So would you like to hear the good news, Luc?"

Luc stood there, clutching his coat closed. How could he sneak by his family and up to his room in the attic above the kitchen?

"Did you get everything you wanted in Sapperton?" Maman asked him when he didn't answer.

Luc nodded. "Here are some Christmas treats for you and the girls." He unloaded his coat pockets onto the table — a big bag of multicoloured candy sticks, another of nuts, and a shiny new ball for Joseph.

"*Ooh!*" Clara cried. "Peppermint sticks! My favourite!"

"What else did you get?" Rita asked. "I can see something there under your coat. A bulge. What is it? What is it? Something for me?"

"No, nothing for you." Everyone was staring at him now. There was no escape. "It's ... um, something for you, Papa. For Christmas." Luc slowly took the package from under his coat. Now he wouldn't even have a chance to wipe it off and fix the strings. "I was going to clean it and oil it, and maybe fix it up for you. Anyway, *Joyeux Noël*, Papa." He thrust the package at his father.

Papa's eyes lit up. "Is this what I think it is?"

Luc held his breath while Papa carefully unwrapped his gift, delicately lifting away the layers of crinkled newspaper.

The violin looked even worse here at home under the quivering oil lamps than it had at Martin's. It was so scratched and dirty that it was hard to see the original colour of the wood.

"I thought we could clean it up and ..." Luc said again. "And you still have the strings from your old violin. And the bow, too, don't you, Papa?"

"Ah, it's seen the wars, this one has. But it's a very good make." Papa thumped the back. "And a good solid instrument."

"I'll get your bow, Papa." Clara ran to their parents' bedroom.

"And your old violin, too." Rita followed her. "I know right where it is in our old trunk."

"Here, you hold it, Luc." Papa laid the instrument on the big kitchen table beside Maman's pastry. "I'll rub a bit of butter on those scratches. There. That looks better already." He pulled out the broken string and installed one from his old violin when Rita brought it for him. "Now here's the real test." He held the violin under his chin and pulled the bow across the strings.

The violin squawked. Luc cringed, and his heart fell. It was no good, after all.

"Just let me tune it up a bit." Papa plucked at the strings, tightened them, and plucked some more. "Now let's try that again."

This time when he drew the bow across the strings the room became filled with a clear, pure note that soon became a rollicking jig. Rita and Clara held hands and danced around and around the room, squealing with delight.

Joseph held up his arms. "Joe-Joe," he said. So they held his hands and danced with him, too, spinning him around and around until they were so dizzy that they all fell into a giggling heap on the floor.

Then Papa switched and played an old French Christmas carol, "Il est né le divin enfant." Maman sang, and so did Luc, harmonizing along. The music filled their little home to bursting. Their new home on the mud flats by the Fraser River.

Luc glanced at Maman and Papa whose grins had become huge smiles of delight. They gazed at him, their eyes shining with pride. Luc thought his heart would explode.

Maman hugged him and said to Papa, "You must tell him the good news now, André, or I'll simply burst."

"Yes, yes." Papa pulled a long, narrow envelope from his jacket pocket. "We received this in the mail, *mon fils*. Something special for you. It's a scholarship to go to the college in New Westminster. A full scholarship for your grade nine. So you will start in January. Both Mr. Rogers and Dr. Scott said it would be a shame if you didn't continue your education. And who knows? Maybe one day you may even become a fine doctor like Dr. Scott."

Luc's head was spinning. "But how will I get there every day? The morning train doesn't get into New Westminster until almost noon."

"Ah, yes!" Papa said. "We thought of that, too. A means of transportation will be very important. Come. We have something else to show you." With that Papa pushed open the kitchen door. And there, leaning against the back porch, was a bicycle!

"A bicycle! For me?" Luc's voice squeaked with excitement. "I can't believe it!"

"Of course, for you. On one condition, though." Papa looked serious.

Luc's heart was beating so hard that he couldn't say anything. He just grinned and nodded and grinned some more. Then he cleared his throat and managed to croak, "Anything, Papa."

"No doubling."

"Of course!" Luc yelped. He straddled the bicycle. It was perfect. Absolutely perfect. In fact, it was a lot like the very bicycle he had seen in the shop months before and had hoped to buy.

"Maybe, as a means of transportation, these newfangled inventions have their place," Papa admitted. "At least you don't have to feed them."

"Or clean up after them!" Rita and Luc said at the same time.